# La Femme Nouvelle

*Limited Autographed Edition*

GIANMARIE

Third Edition Copyright © 2022 GIANMARIE
Kairos Moment Publishing Group
Minneapolis, MN
All rights reserved

ISBN: 9798458436151

*I dedicate this collection to my legacy, the light of my life, my son-shine.
Pursue your dreams with your natural curiosity, firm resolve & tenacity.*

# AUTOGRAPH MESSAGE

*Share your love & light in the world!*

*Peace,*
*GianMarie C.H.*

# CONTENTS

| | |
|---|---|
| AUTOGRAPH MESSAGE | i. |
| CONTENTS | iii. |
| FOREWORD | 1 |
| BLACK GIRL DAYDREAMIN | 3 |
| DEEPER HUES OF RED | 21 |
| DARKER SHADES OF BLUE | 47 |
| A STILL QUIET MOMENT | 63 |
| POETIC ENTICEMENT | 105 |
| RETURN PASSAGE | 165 |
| POET'S CORNER | 205 |

# FOREWORD

In this anthology of over 100 collected poems, *La Femme Nouvelle* takes the reader on a personal renaissance of womanhood over three decades in the making. Readers traverse the globe with poet GianMarie as she connects with her tribe on a Pan-Afrikan journey across the diaspora.

The movement continues to evolve in the U.S. as well, redefined by societal highs including eight years of the first black president, black billionaires & women winning at just about everything; to the deepest, soul-crushing lows brought on by the endless suffering of black & brown skin at the hands of police brutality, the resurgence of white supremacy & voter oppression. All while society fights to survive a worldwide pandemic that has added more back breaking weight to the already oppressive economic instability of the American Dream.

If, *Black Girl Daydreamin* is a subtle whisper, then *Soul Anthropology* is the poet's primal cry. GianMarie speaks her truth in this collection by saying, "The era of the polite negro masses has passed. No longer shall we be pacified, silenced or dismissed."

In this anthology of her written work thus far, GianMarie asserts her raw, non sugar-coated existence through her poetry. Wise words offer food for thought. GianMarie offers *La Femme Nouvelle* to satiate the edacious soul. Meet the renewed woman.

# BLACK GIRL DAYDREAMIN
*Poems for flight of the imagination.*

*Muse*

Quietly follow me
Shadow in the full moonlight
Exhale whispers
Through my amber curls
A warm breeze teasing me
In the coolness of night
Inhale my heavy sweetness
Become intoxicated

Spy me walking
Through trees of forest green
Photograph my frame
Etch my curves into memory

Peer through the swaying willows
Join me as I prepare to bathe
In a bubbling hot spring
See the steam curls gently kiss
My golden skin
Submerge into vapors
Come explore my secret world within

Take brush to canvas
Stroke me new life
Capture my essence in ink
With paper begin to write
Seduce me with your magic words

Drift sweetly to sleep
Dream me
Free as a mare running wild
Through the grassy plains of your mind

Imagine me
The one you adore
Enraptured by love
Imagine you & I
Entangled blissfully
Becoming more
Imagine, *we*.

Sincerely,

Your Muse

*Smile (stay awhile)*
Your smile glistens
Bright as the morning sun
Just begun

Your eyes twinkle
Shining as the moonlight
Full in the night

Laugh, laugh
Roll around with me
In the grasses
Under swaying trees
Smell the green scents
Summer's best
No contest

Sleep, sleep
Lay with me
Hand in arm
Leg on knee

Rest, rest
On me
Soothed by the heartbeat
In my breast
Loving my sweet caress

Stay, stay
Be with me always
As the seasons change
Our love remains the same.

*Playful*
Heat
D
r
i
p
p
i
n
g
Down me
My spine
Curves
In
&
Out
Round
&
Round
You in me
Steam vapors
Rising
To the ceiling
Kisses raise the hairs on my neck
Tickle, tickle causing a giggle
To escape past the smile on my face
You are
Beautiful
You are
Sensual
You are
You
It's wonderful
A spell cast over we

Eternally
My lover & me.

*Visions*

I close my eyes
My mind wanders in a dream
We are on an island
The sun is beaming heat
All over everything
We relax in the cool shade of swaying palm trees
White sand warms our feet
Submerged
Smiling
Our minds are at peace
Bright rays dance
Against your shoulders
Tanned from the beach
You laugh at something I say
Your gentle eyes sparkle back at me
I close my eyes
Inhaling the salty sea breeze
Listening
The palm leaves begin to speak
The waves
Beating the shore
Rhythmically like a heartbeat.

I open my eyes
We are in a basement parlor
I can hear a mixture of bustling activity
From the street above
A backdrop
To the jazz band playing
Something blue
Cool & laid back on the beat
Candles flicker
Light dances on their wicks

To the music
I snap my fingers
Tapping my feet
You smile lazily at me
The bass line walks up & down
Our heads nod slowly
I'm caught gazin at you
When the sax blazes a solo
Causing my heart to skip a beat
Yeah, play brotha play!
Music & you generates such heat
We sway to the song
Driftn in relaxation/
My love for you is/ driftin in
Relaxation, driftin in
My love is for you.

*Stardust*

\* Once in a blue moon \*
\* A guardian shines golden in the dusk \*
\* The Son's heated touch \*
\* Paints the night sky in blush \*
\* Stardust glistens in his eyes \*
\* Its sparkle causing my warmth to rise \*
\* My thighs quiver as his thoughts linger \*
\* Over my mind \*
\* Making me wonder \*
\* How he does this every time \*
\* In the night \*
\* I search the cosmos \*
\* For my blue moon delight \*
\* Longing for \*
\* Needing, craving the haunting \*
\* Of his celestial love \*
\* Daunting is my wait \*
\* For a sign from above \*
\* When the sky shows \*
\* Traces of red & pink lace \*
\* I eagerly await my angelic mate \*
\* To sprinkle my soul \*
\* In star dusted fate. \*

*La Habana*

Cuba, el sol y mar, how lovely is she
The Cubanos are as beautiful as
The fertile land that birthed them
The morena island
A small piece of heaven

The countryside is abundant
Life springing forth from
God's richest blood
Providing the purest of fruits
As a mother to her sons

I find an empty bench strolling along El Malecon
I sit & gaze into the Caribbean Sea
Tropical melodies the birds sing to me
The bustling city disappears as the warm salty breeze
Kisses my eyelids to sleep
The shady fronds of palm trees
Reach down to cover me

This land
When she speaks, she shouts
When she cries, she wails
When Cuba smiles her people rejoice
Right now her laughter is all around me.

*Secret Garden*
I find myself walking
In the summer night
Through jasmine scented fog
Lit by golden light

As the smoke clears slowly
To my surprise I see
The sparkle of the moon
In your eyes looking at me

Feet sink into softness
One step at a time
The cool of dew kissed moss
Sends shivers up my spine

Suddenly you appear
Under a large oak tree
Your arms like its branches
Beckon out to me

The warmth of your breath
Exhaled from our embrace
Gently finds my neck
Quickening my heart's pace

Leading with familiar comfort
Your fingers linked in mine
I wonder if we were lovers
In another place & time

As we meet in secret
While no one is aware
The wind exchanges whispers

While the whole world disappears.

*Fantasy*

Close your eyes & listen
To the cottonwood trees
Their shimmering leaves
Sound like waves on the beach
So calming & soothing
You're drifting to sleep...

We're exploring an island
In the shade of palm trees
The warmth of white sand
Radiates under bare feet

We find an empty yacht
Anchored quiet & clean
Excited we board
Deciding to break free

Sailing through the day
On gem colored seas
Until the sun sets
Casting purples & pinks

The gentle bob of the ocean
Rocks us into the night
As we lay baring all
Under the pale moonlight

My soft skin tingles
In the palms of your hands
Exploring in composure
Despite fire within

Teasing me with kisses

I'm unable to think
We succumb when our desire
Reaches its brink
Into a whirlwind of passion
We happily sink

In the night we dream
Of love flying free
Soaring under the stars
Above rippling sea

We leave the cool waters
For the warmth of dense trees
Floating through a chorus
Of animals unseen

We navigate in darkness
Led by the jasmine scent
Of a babbling stream
Into jagged mountains
With cloud covered peaks

Nearing the thundering roar
Of water falling from cliffs
We duck through its shower
Tingling from the cool mist
Sheltered in a secret chamber
Of smooth polished rock
The beating of water
Causes us to nod off...

We awake to your bed
Wrapped in a warm embrace
Legs & arms entangled

As we lay face to face
No intrusions by the phone
No one else to share our space
We love the day away
To the sound of drumming rain.

*Les Francais*

You smoke everywhere
No matter what the sign says
Unbothered, you don't care
You work to live
Happy hour never ends
You will sleep when you're dead
The purplish circle under eye
In the morning tells no lie
L'aperitif is red wine
With fries on the side
You buy roasted chicken from a cart
For dessert apple tart
With sarcasm you argue & fuss
Laugh then kiss & make up
You curse when you sing
Without worry, C'est la vie!
You don't care, you're unaware
You leave a perfumed trail in the air
You bump other cars as you park
You bump against people when you walk
Bumping for you is a national art
You wear two scarves when it's not cold
When asked why you reply, C'est la mode!
You rush along a cobblestone path
In the shade of a floppy hat
You are the center of everything
Your shirt reads, New York Loves Me!
Without apology
You are The French.

*Daydreamin*
Butterflies flutter
Their delicate wings
Dusting my lashes
Until I barely see

Yellow rays shine
Warmly kissing my cheeks
Sending currents of heat
All over me

A cool breeze teases
Its fingers through my hair
Caresses so light
I'm barely aware

Stars that sparkle
In your eyes
Have this power
To hypnotize

The imagined touch
Of your electric hand
Against my skin
Causes a shudder deep within

Why do I smile
For no reason other than
The thought of you
Entering in my head.

# DEEPER HUES OF RED
*Poems of the heart & soul.*

*I See You*
I see you
The god in you
A light in your eyes
Your soul shining through
Sparkling diamonds in sunlight
Your heart is a precious stone
If I could just get through
The wall surrounding you
That is holding love captive
In hardened rock
Imprisoned is the beauty within
How I long to release
Your beauty within

I see you
Silky smooth is your touch
The feel of your fingers
Lightly tracing my skin
Up & down my curves
Melting gold into liquid
With every stroke you adore
Even softer are your kisses
Telling me to calm my fear
Drawing me closer & closer
To venture inside
Deeper & deeper
Where the lion resides

I see you
Since I was a little girl
Too shy to meet you
To speak to the god
I worshiped in secret

Dreaming of both day & night
How I wanted you
Longed for you to take a bite
To take possession of my soul
As I peered at you in the hallways
Through classroom doors
A foolish young girl I was,
Ready to be a fool for your love.

*Love Stories*
A flutter
Barely noticeable
Somewhere deep
Deeply forgotten
Unknown
Unrecognizable
Begins to spread
Warmth from the inside out
Tingling
Vibrations
All around
A smile
My chest fills
Feels excitement
My stomach contracts
Tightening
With anticipation
As the haze clears
A single thought
Enlightenment!
I cannot eat
I cannot breathe
I cannot think
Of anything but you
New Love.

Heat
Sizzling
All over me
Burning, churning, turning
Layers of rock into liquid
Around my heart
So hopeful
So willing to give
Freely the best of me
So ready
To ignore, deny, even lie
To shadow the shortcomings
Emotion so deep
Never felt before
Never imagined
With all my creative power
Would love devour
This must be
This must be it
The "it" they talk about
What they write about
With no end in sight
I will not see
I will not be
Without you
Young Love.

Comfort is found in your voice
Your eyes penetrate me
Knowing
Showing
That you see
The things unspoken in me
You know laughter
You know tears
You know my fears
I don't have to wonder
Wandering alone in life's desert
You are there
My oasis
You will forever be
So deeply planted beneath my skin
I feel you
As I feel myself
Unshakable, uncontrollable, undeniable
It does not matter
The choices you made
The life you lead
Closer or further from me
I can share
Because it's always there
Old Love.

I see you
An apple dangling from a tree
Shining ripe & juicy
Your curves seduce me
Beckoning me
To come closer
To linger
To reach out
Feel the luster of your skin
Plucking you from limb to limb
Biting, ingesting, inhaling
Tasting your bittersweet fruit
You quench this need
This raw aching desire
The fire long gone
Leaving nothing but dry
Withered bone
A dust only you alone
Can bring life to
But you don't belong
To me
To taste your wonders is a trespass
That would yield only pain
Your pleasures will have to remain
My torturer, my tempter, my mystery
Forbidden Love.

*Blacklight (oxymoron)*
Dark & lovely, moreno, cho-co-late
Caramel, cream, cocoa, coffee
Cappuccino-delight
Mocha, molasses, purple, blue, ebony...

NAW! Jus give me tha blackest man
So we can unite & make tha blackest
Most passionate, midnight love
So out of my womb we create
Tha blackest babies
Tha universe has eva seen
Makin "I Have a Dream," seem like reality

I want a man so black
White goes color blind
A man so black night seems like day
Turning darkness to light
I wanna man so black
Tha sun looks cold
Makin molten lava turn frozen & old

I wanna man so black
Creation saw betta days
So black the earth trembles & quakes
Thinkin tha Father has returned
To proclaim His reign

I wanna man so black
That shadows cease
As black as the richest soil after it rains
His seeds growing to be
Tha strongest Kings & Queens
Ruling, leading, setting a way

So powerful evil is held at bay

I wanna man so black
Beauty forgets her name
These words written in black ink
Simply fade away.

## *Could It Be*

W O W
Ooooo
Could it be you
Stirring somethin inside me brand new
You, you, you
With your beautiful words
Have given me thoughts
So strange & absurd
Like meeting you, touching you
Lost in those eyes
Your words mesmerize
Igniting flames in my thighs

You, you, you
Cause civil unrest
There is no precedence
For the flava you attest
Mmm, mmm, mmm
The taste of love in my mouth
How I wish to spill it out
Scream & shout
Let it sprout
A piece of you
Its roots embedded deep within

You
In
Me
No, no, no
It could never be
For you are a stranger I saw on a screen
So. . .
You, you, you

A pixel memory
Something buzzing inside of me
A fleeting honey bee
Attracted to the soft & sticky.

~

Sweet sexy butta brown
Milky chocolate melted down
Too hot to touch, as the sun comes round
Burning lust neva causin a frown
Love vibrations in surround sound
Words electric & so profound
Essence not captured nor bound
With eyes wide open, lost is now found

Thank you,
For showing me
For being free
For could it be.

*Soulful*
I lay at night thinking
Drifting to sleep
Dreaming dreams of you
When I awake there you are still
Never leaving me

So full, *Soulful*, so full of soul you are
I look into your eyes
I see the pain of a thousand disappointments
I see the frustration
I also see love where anger died
I see strength in place of fear
I see your light shining through

*Soulful*, you carry the weight of the world
On your shoulders
Trying to provide for so much need
You don't desire
Aspire for many things
Your heart grows big from the memory
Of what it was to be hungry
With nowhere to eat

You know life can be lonely
In your greatest time of need
You know pain
You know loss
You have lived the darkness
Suffocating, surrounded by it
Its walls closing in

*Soulful*, so full of soul you are
Your compassion makes you strong

Keep giving, keep caring
Keep sharing love
Call on Him when it becomes too much
Call on Him when no hand
Nor mouth turns up
Call on Him in your need

*Soulful*, your time for hurt
Your time for lack
Your time to be broken is over
When you are ready for wisdom
To understand in full
Go to Him
Bring it to Him
Lay it at His feet

So full, *Soulful*, so full of soul you are
Always there at the forefront of my thoughts
In my heart so deep you penetrate to levels
I only feel but cannot see
You awaken life in me
So full of purpose is your walk
Your destiny
I will not ask you to pause
Along your path to wait for me

*Soulful*, as you draw nearer
Closer to that perfect peace
I will meet you there
Kneeling at His feet.

*I Wish*

I wish I
Could cuddle up with you all day
Gaze into your eyes
Til stars come out & play

I wish I
Could run my fingers
Up & down your back
Kiss your lips
Sipping love extract

I wish I...
I wish I could...
Need you
More than the air I breathe
Want you
More than my drive to succeed
Hold you
To me closer than the blood I bleed
Feel you
In every heartbeat
I wish
I could
Let go
Be your everything.

*Desire*
Use me
Abuse me
For your amusement
Choose me
Beat me like a drum
Swallow me whole
Chug me like a barrel of rum
Break me
Tear me apart
Rip me into shreds
Despise me
Chastise me
Take all that I am
Leave nothing left to love
Leave nothing left love
Desire
Why is it that you consume me so.

*Sometimes*

Underneath angel wings
What does it mean
To have you hold me
Sometimes I wonder

Sippin on warm cocoa
Steam rolls off my lips
Warm chocolate lover
Mmm I feel slumber
Coming over me
Driftin in a dream

Whipped cream & strawberries
Sweet tease will you please
Pass me some good lovin

All night long
I lay wondering why
I crave you by my side
With your arms encircling me
Keeping me alive
As a queen bee keeps her hive
Sweet honey kept warm inside
Me & you
Sometimes I wonder

I love to be alone
Gray stormy days
I gaze out glass window panes
Into rainy haze
Or am I looking at a mirror
Reflecting inner turmoil
Sometimes I wonder. . .

Always straying
Forever laying
With new princes
Dreamin of becoming
My one & only king
I am not satisfied
My soul continues to wander
Aimlessly sometimes.

*Yours*

Undeniable
My thoughts of you
Turning to sweet dreams every night
Your love haunts me
As a thief taking every part of me
That does not want you
To be with me
Need to
Belong to you
Love you
To breathe
Look into my eyes
Show me everything is alright
Calm whisperings relax me
Giving my soul peace

Unchangeable
I am yours
Because I cannot remember
A life without you
I cannot hope for a time beyond you
My path is forever intertwined with yours
Love grows as a vine
That will not allow us to part
Entangling fates
The new rhythm of my heart beats
I love
You
I am
Yours.

*Found*
Strangely
Just under the surface
A feeling lives
Yearning, turning, churning
Morphing into somethin more
What starts as a random thought
Becomes a faint memory
Like a dream
You wake from slowly
Unable to shake
Or fully recall
Then suddenly
It's there
Growing bigger
Living in the back of your mind
Causing you to lose focus
Lose track of time
Unable to sleep
You lay awake at night
Staring through the ceiling
Searching the universe
There is no escape
From the feeling
That something is missing
The hollow in your heart
Making you not quite right
You go on day & night
Robotic, incomplete
You are not the same
People ask if you're okay
When the old jokes
Bring no smile to your face
When the old routine

Now seems so strange
You are changed
A voice inside tells you
To calm your fear
Do not despair
You check yourself
Everything is still there
Relaxing
You hear, "peace be still"
Then you begin to see
This whole time
You've been wondering
What was wrong with you
What has gone from you
One day
Just like any other
You wake up to find
The sun shines a lil brighter
Your heart feels a lil lighter
The smells you inhale
Awaken your spirit again
Expectation
Your skin tingles
As you check your email
There's a knock at the door
Read a text
Open a letter
You hear the phone ring
Finally
A smile creeps in
You realize
You are not losing your mind
What you sought after
You now easily find

The missing element
In your life
Was me.

I whisper in your ear,
"I've been looking
for so long
not knowing I was lost
until I found you."

## *Agape*

Like I never knew sorrow
I found my tears
Like I never spoke a word
I found my voice
Like I never felt human
I found my heart
As I looked into your eyes
I found my meaning for life
To Serve You.

### *Mother To Child*

My babies
My sons
My daughters of this earth
Love will survive

In life there are lessons
Learning makes us wise
After all dust settles
Love will rise

Take courage
Stand up!
Be comforted in trials
Let love thrive

In the river of life
Change is a constant current
Be strong, be rock
Keep love alive.

*Inauguration*

Rise, rise my people
Lift your weary eyes
Awake to these changed times
We never hoped to see
Realized in our lives

Sing, sing my sistas
Let love spring forth
From lips of joy
Laughing as tears
Bathe the ancestors
Buried deep within

Stretch, stretch my brothas
Give forth a helping hand
Lift up your fellow man
Recognizing in him
Reflections of the great I Am

Dream, dream my children
Release your imaginations
Into the wind
Seeds of limitless ambition
For our future begins
With His inauguration!

## *If It Has Been Spoken*

Can I get an Amen!
If it has been spoken
Then let it be written
A token of my faith
The Spirit of righteousness
Longs for better days

In May spring flowers bloom
My skin prickles from melanin
Awakening again
From the sun's warm rays
Something bout summer comin
Mellows my ways

However, sons & daughters of the One
We cannot sleep in these latter times
We cannot creep
Ashamed to proclaim His name

Sing bout yonder all you want
You won't be leaving
Til your work is done
Are you ready for the Father to come

From darkness to the dawn
Don't be caught sleepin
On your Son-rise
Your job is to open your brotha's eyes

Sistas! Do not be mislead
To compromise
Morality for vanity
Giving into temporary insanity

If it has been spoken
Then let it be written
Til all time ends
Peace.

# DARKER SHADES OF BLUE
*Poems that speak to the human condition.*

*Victimization*

How can you eat?
How dare you speak
Don't look at me

Pretend to be a friend
While your manipulation
Knows no end

Patting me on the back
Laughing
Smiling smugly

I feel neither peace nor happiness
Only grief as I weep
In anger that has no release

Do not intellectualize my suffering
With your silver lining
In attempt to console

My relief from torment only comes
After you have paid your toll
With your soul

Only then
Will the legacy
Of victimization end.

*Katutura*

See me, SEE ME
Look at me I plead
Comfort me & mine
For all the times
You turned your cheek
Blind to me

Hear me, HEAR ME
The words long overdue
Internalized wounds,
You cut me
I bleed
Not just me
Thousands bled
Now long dead
In unmarked graves
It's time for a change

Feel me, FEEL ME
Pain deep inside
Not for one moment you abide
Afraid to touch
What you created inside.

*Rage*
Hate
Grows in me
Fuels the fire
Burning in me
A cycle that began in you
Now consumes me
Eats away my flesh
Leaves me feeling
Powerless
Unable to withstand
It defeats me in the end
Hate kills me
Now I am dead

Silence
I want to scream!
Blindness
I want to see
Hate imprisons me (my psyche)
But I long to be free.

*Missed*

How is it that I missed you
I met you a bit too late
You are committed to another
So there goes our fate
Back to the clouds & stars
Where our creator decides
The rising sun & changing moon tides

How is it that I can't forget you
As much as I've tried
To say that I don't want to
Is a bold faced lie
I could die tomorrow
You'd still be on my mind

Every crossing is meant
Pieces of a larger design
But this one just boggles my mind
Is the point to appreciate each moment
Those in it & those to come
Or just to remind me
Who I have is no one.

## *Soweto*

I WANT TO SCREAM
RUN RAMPANT
RIP & TEAR
TIL ALL IS BARE
WHITE
ARE MY KNUCKLES
CLENCHED IN FISTS
FURY, FURY
BURY ME DEEP
DON'T LET A SINGLE WHITE LIGHT SEEP
IN TO REACH ME

You do not want to see
My anger unleashed
That is why
After centuries of brutality
Now you speak of peace
You teach, you preach
But what was it you practiced
On me & those before me?

Come out, come out
Set the truth free
Or bury deep
Me & my fury.

*Disconnected Confusion*
I feel confused, disoriented
Unsettled in my ways
I enter a daze to lighten my spirit
Calm my soul
I feel not of the earth sometimes
I just want to look into your eyes

No sound but the rainfall
No chatter from the hall
Simple pleasant creation of a mellow mood
An escape from a world that can be so rude
I see the derealization
Of people's shattered lives
Now I just want to look into your eyes

Tonight I seek relief from pain
Breathing slowly trying to settle my mind
All loneliness would end
With one touch of your hand

Behind closed eyes I feel your breath
Against my temple
As you whisper sweet things
Quickening my heartbeat

How can I make you understand
I wish I were lead sinking into the ocean
Of your love sometimes...
I just want to look into your eyes

I grow weary instead
I feel expired like stale bread
When will this relentless separation end

Why can't I
How I long to
Please allow me
One more time
I am your feign openly in the daylight
I just want to look into your eyes

The strongest communication
Is found within those pupils
The kind of closeness that keeps me alive
I pause, remembering the last time
I looked into your beautiful brown eyes

Elevated
I return to a normal state of mind
Reconnected
I linger suspended in time
How wonderful it is to gaze into your eyes
Even if it is only
In the meditations of my mind.

*Legacy*

I drink, I smoke
Why I damage myself
I do not know
I try to suppress
The anguish & pain
Caused purposely
To drain
The life from me

I scream, I scheme
I deal & steal
Sometimes I even rape & kill
Why I do it, unknown still
Jus actin out da anger inside that I feel

My lack of pride
A growing tide of fury
Buried, ingrained so deep in me
Seeping through the cracks
Tearing to come out
Erupting on those all around
My loved ones, my friends
Or strangers with dark skin

Victims by my hands
Still I'm unable to understand
This was never my plan
But I cannot reach, or see
Who did this to me

I know nothing else
My inner turmoil
Expressed in violence

The process, the poison
The system
I continue to pay the cost

The Master's plan
Is still my boss.

### *In Just a Day*

In just a day
I felt complete happiness
Then devastating pain

In just a day
I went from being asleep
To fully awake

In just a day
You were my sunshine
Then my torrential rain

In just a day
I was love
Then loved in vain

In just a day
I went from first to last

In just a day
I had all I could take

In just a day
In just a day
In just one day
My everything changed
What a difference a day makes.

### *Void*

I don't know who I am no mo
I've lost myself in you completely
My mind does not see
Its own identity
Every day is the same
Creativity washed down the drain
Whose thoughts are those
Words expressed so dryly
The universe is you
I am but a dim star in the distance
Surrounded by your void
Mindless thoughts of nothingness
But you are not the sun
Keeping my planet alive
Because there is nothing bright about you
Your vast emptiness
Swallows all light
That might have come from me
There is no hope
I am but a fragment, a half thought
In your black hole of loneliness
Gravity- your charm
Pulled me into this trap
Your emptiness disoriented me
Now I am lost
More alone than ever
I no longer recognize who I am, where I be.

*I Need You*
Desperate & alone
I feel as empty as a clone
Without you
Not even blue
But a gloomy shade of gray
Thundering clouds
Not a single drop of rain
I am barren as the desert in my pain
You were my oasis
I grow weak as a hummingbird
Without loves pollen
My soul has fallen
Into a dangerous abyss of unhappiness
Since our last kiss
The memory brings on no bliss
Because shortly after
My love you did dismiss
A bittersweet diss
Throwing daggers at my heart
You told me you didn't need my love
Slowly losing my grip
In my desperation I am alone
Empty as a clone
Now you are gone
My heart is a broken record
Repeating on & on & on.

### *It's Complicated*

My mind swings on a pendulum
Back & forth with no end
Understanding dizzied by the momentum
My lover or best friend
Unable to see clearly
Right from wrong
What I need & want
Singing to each other
Sad love songs
One over the other
I cannot choose
The perfect mate
If both were embodied in one
Reconciled into something
Sustainable
Unable to prioritize
Day or night
Dark or light
They complement each other
They compete with one another
For my attention
My time is the currency of trade
All this push & pull
Slowly driving me insane
Leaving me emotionally bankrupt
Without one
The other is not enough
Don't make me choose
Don't make me choose!
In the end only I will lose
Everything
I know the time is coming
For the other hand to drop

An emailed note
Late night phone call
An ultimatum
Even I will be surprised
Which one first severs the ties
Blurry is the line
Between commitment & free
The one I chose first
Or the one whom first chose me
Where lies my loyalty
Unable to renege
On so many promises made
Over the years
Now my only fear is discovery
My destiny
Maybe they will both decide to leave
Rejected I will be
Without the warmth of my lover
Nor the console of my friend.

## *Twisted*

Life has a twisted humor
I feel the universe laughing at my dream
The vision of your love sustaining me
So long I wanted to express love freely
Waiting in the wings
Patiently as your friend
For the time to be just right
For love to be
Aligned with the universe
Changing with the tides
A delusional notion of bliss
Our little piece of happiness
Just when my heart had enough
Of my love's futility
There you were suddenly free
Dedicating your love to me
But I had already given my heart away
Now you wait in desperate vain
For the day to come when love is free again
Steadily putting visions in my head
Enticing me with your words
Heavy in weight but empty in meaning
Because you do not belong to me
Not then, not now, not ever
Please stop dedicating your love to me
Pledging how you will wait for me
We were never meant to be
More than each other's twisted fantasy.

# A STILL QUIET MOMENT
*Poems on a healing journey.*

### *I Love Us*

Just like you
I walked to da corner store
In bibs denim blue
Wearing nike shoes
Sporting twists & braids
Sippin quarter grape soda
At the community pool

All seeds sown in the same soil
Fed by the sun
How we grow no one knows
I love us

Just like you
Dressed in thrift store finds
Dreaming of something new
When we outgrew
Hand me downs now they're cut offs
I sat by mamas stove
With the hot comb too close to my neck
Called it the crisco press

All seeds sown in the same soil
Fed by the sun
How we grow no one knows
I love us

Just like you
I played hopscotch
From squares of chalk
Jumped double dutch
Ran after the ice cream truck
Bomb pops til my tongue was blue

When the street light came on
Time to head indoors

All seeds sown in the same soil
Fed by the sun
How we grow no one knows
I love us

Just like you
Auntie out back in the garden
Peeled taters & pickled peppers
Breaking stems off green beans
Red Kool Aid in ice cube trays
Toothpick pops cool the tongue on hot summer days
Laying under the oak tree for shade
Day dreaming of better days

All seeds sown in the same soil
Fed by the sun
How we grow no one knows
I love us.

## *Caged Bird*

Freedom
Starts as a faint whisper
Muttered almost inaudibly
In the dewy haze of my mind
Bars, wrought iron & faded
Paint chips of white
All that is left of former beauty
Mangled, twisting & turning
As a vine of ivy crawling upward
Reaching for the promise of light
The warmth of a sun not felt
Mocking my confinement
The smell of stale dust hangs in the air
Leaving no hope for release
Have I ever felt a warm breeze
The invigorating sensation as it ruffles through my feathers
My wings creak of dry bone
From an overturned & long forgotten water bowl
Years have slowly melded together into
One indistinguishable thought
That I can no longer recall
The silence, long suffering gives way
To a single word
That slowly burns in my belly
Reminding me how it feels to be alive
What it is to hunger & thirst
A yearning triggered in my chest
Quickens my heart
Gathering the strength
To once more fight
Against the quicksand of time
My senses tingle as they vibrate
Through my old tired body

Firing a message to my brain
A singular thought
Awaken!

*I was dreaming for so long*
*Of a life well lived & now gone*
*In this life I knew struggle & felt pain*
*I loved*
*Was heart broken & loved again*
*I had friends come & go*
*Many places I traveled*
*To receive recognition & praise*
*For the wisdom I knew*
*I laughed & played*
*Danced & prayed*
*Ate meals prepared by the finest chefs*
*Slept in the softest of beds*
*Life vibrated through me*
*I gave of myself*
*All that I am & left nothing undone*
*I sang a song.*

I awaken from my dream
To a cage that I realize
Is too small to contain me
I remember what it is to feel desire
I long to be free
The word rises within me
A small whisper grows into a shout
FLY!

I stand up tall
Steady the creaking bones in my legs
To support my withered body

The bars shake beneath me
I inhale deeply
Stagnant air burns in my nostrils
Stretching my shrunken lungs
My eyes blink away the fog
From too many days long gone
Revitalized by the idea of hope
I shake my feathers
The cage shudders & moans
The door creaking on a rusty hinge
Swings slowly open
No longer can I be held captive
For the cage was in my mind
I remember who I am

My morning song,
"Carry me, wind of change, come carry me away."
I sing as I rise, & rise, & rise into glory!
I am freedom
In that moment the sun breaks over a mountain
The warm breeze of dawn greets outstretched wings
This is the day the caged bird flew away.
*-Rest in power Maya*

*Queen*
Musical royalty
You sing
You sting
Moaning, groaning
You feed this need
Your songs, notes strong
Weep tears of blood
Speak of love long gone
You please
You tease
Numbing my pain
Your melodies are a healing rain

Beat your black drum
Rhythms da dum dum
I sway
Staying in your midst
All day
Stuck on replay
Neva will I wake
From this dreamy haze
Your artistry
Neva ceases to amaze
Your grace
Your ebony face
Turned to the sky
Reflecting moonlight
Sweetly, deeply

Melancholy takes me
As you sing:
Just like a woman
To be young gifted & black

Wild as the wind
Summertime
Since I fell for you
My funny valentine
I want a little sugar in my bowl
Take me to the water
I'm feelin good.
*-Rest in power Nina*

## *Bad Habit*

Every bit of me needs him
Every part of me tries to deny
Why, I never asked for this
I never desired to give my power away
I never expected my resistance to be so easily diminished
I never invited him to take over my mind

It would be so much easier to give in to him
Let the fire simmering beneath skin breathe again
Grow stronger with fresh oxygen
To possess & be possessed even more
In the arms of one another
The calm before the storm
That becomes a perfect still moment
To lose oneself in the abyss
The only reminder of time passing
Is the slow & steady beating of hearts

I won't let him go
I live in such hypocrisy
I am not fully aware of why
I am older
I am wiser
With less tolerance for foolery
No matter how long love lasts
It always ends the same
Blood, sweat, & tears pouring like rain

I am past the age of not caring
Ignoring the coming pain
Something about this feels different
Than my normal desire & intrigue
There is no one like him

He delves deeper inside
Past the layers & failsafes
His technique is artistry
There is no chance of survival
Total system meltdown beyond recovery

The stakes are higher now
I have more to lose than ever before
Gone is the innocence of our youthful bond
Stripped from us
Is the sweet fragrance of blissful ignorance
That fills our senses
Ending too quickly
Leaving us craving more

I would drown in sorrow for him
I have sipped the spirit of love lost
Choked on its bitterness
Every time he walks away
Leaving my head spinning
Feigning for his taste

I punish lesser men
Crushing fragile egos
With white hot rage
In wrathful fury for him leaving
My vengeance reclaiming lost power
Tender hearts I devour
Consuming their vitality
To recover
It is all for nothing
He returns to find me defenseless
Unwilling to resist him

We share this fantasy
Calmly coexisting in a peaceful place
We imagine bringing out the best in each other
If being tamed was the only consequence of loving him
Then I would willingly surrender
Trading freedom to welcome bliss
For some reason I know it doesn't exist
No gentleness awaits
No healing reconciliation

Between us
Violence we always choose
There would be brutality
I can feel the fire that waits to consume
I see the vapors rising
From the heat that our closeness emanates
Ashes & dust
All that's left of our love
When the cipher completes
Back to the origin
Until the cycle repeats

I'm ready for something different
It's time for healing
I resolve to follow my conviction
To lock the vault surrounding my heart
Blocking entry to lustful toxicity
The only thing that hurts more
Than life without his love
Is the certain death of self that results.

## *Soul Tie*

Once I experienced passion overflowing
With someone who loved with his whole being
Holding nothing back he gave love freely
Without him feels like something is missing

Since I have learned that one can only love
From the capacity his heart is capable of
No matter how much you pour in
He cannot reciprocate beyond his limits within

Like sea water in a desert land
I drink but my thirst is never quenched
The more I partake the more desperate my need
Until the mirage fades revealing its salinity

What's wrong
Nothing & everything

It is so difficult
To remain rooted in the present
When the heart is not receiving
Nourishing fulfillment

He's giving me his everything
Yet it's only a fraction of what I used to receive
The love that flowed so readily
Between you & me fulfilling every need

Our love was so easy I mistook it for regular
Now I realize it was extraordinarily rare
It kills my heart to compare
Leading me down a dark road of despair

What's wrong
Nothing & everything

I try desperately to be content with new love
Only to find that my heart is a bottomless cup
He pours in what he has to give
Every passing day I grow more unfulfilled

Just when my heart has suffered
All the emotional neglect it can take
Here he comes acting selflessly
Reminding me why I chose this fate

What's wrong
Nothing & everything

He's given me the world & a beautiful life
Always there for the important times
He's denied me nothing my heart desires
Except the kind of love that sets my soul afire

Our love came so easily
I took for granted that it would never leave
I know that impossible choices were made
I still long for the love you gave

Will I ever be able to move beyond
The passion we created when love was young
I only wish that I would have stayed
Cherishing the perfect love we made.

*Enough*

It is so hard to love you
To penetrate
The fortress that surrounds you
So guarded
So afraid to trust
That love is enough
To keep me from leaving
Giving up on us
The moment times get rough

It is hard to
Give light to
Your darkest fears
To comfort you
Soothe the aching pain
Embedded deep
In your DNA
A baby thrown away
The eternal orphan
Stepped over
Left behind
Unwanted & afraid
Until your heart hardened enough
To silence the pain

I give you all of me
It is never enough
To fill the void others drained
Yet I keep pouring
Keep adoring
Soothing
Loving
Warming

Caressing
With tender patience
Every inch that you open
Letting me in
Just a little
For the win

Enough to keep me hoping
Wishing
Dreaming
Planning
For a future
A family
A home full of joy

Our love is calm & quiet
We never choose violence
Instead we shut the world out
Laugh & cuddle
We stay in all weekend
In a sun-filled kitchen
Saturday mornings cooking breakfast
Flipping hotcakes in your boxers
Vibing to Isley Brothers

On rainy days
We burn one & snuggle
Finding comfort in our bare skin
We relax & lay playing footsie
Warming ourselves in black satin sheets
We love hard
Kissing softly
Constant tug of war
More & more

Over & over
Again & again
Skin dripping sweat
Tangled hair sprawled all over the bed

We never tire of us
Incense burning
Smoke dances all around
Voyage to Atlantis
We groove to the sound
Bodies in unison
Winding, twisting, grinding
Losing track of time
Until light slips into darkness
We dream transported
By love's sweet tonic

It is never enough
Every progress
Ignites a burning fear
In your inner child
To run
To hide
Whenever your door opens wide
You slam it shut
Lock me out
Starve me of tenderness
Punishment for loving you too much

Back to zero
We start over
Try again
Hoping the cycle will finally end
Just let go

You can trust me
You have me
I offer freely
All that I am

It is so hard to love you
I starve to feed you
Filling you up
Until I am running on dust
Still not enough
Self-fulfilling prophecy
I make plans to quit us
Now you're on bended knee
Begging me to stay
Visions of a wedding day
Desperate words
Too little too late
Feeling so betrayed
You shatter our picture frame
Cutting yourself
In a fit of rage
No fight left in me today
There's nothing left to say

Taking time for healing
The only life I crave
Is one that gives love freely
Building instead of taking
More of me each day
Still remnants of you remain
Haunting my dreams

My heart flutters
When I see your pretty face

Soft waves of black hair
Gathered at your neck's nape
Almond eyes shining under long lashes
Squinted in a silly grin
Flashing pearly whites
Against caramel skin

I wish it were untrue
Lord knows I don't want to
Love you again
I awake from your visits amazed
By my heart's fidelity
Although I'll never let you back in
My love remains unchanged.

*Altered Fate: a short story*
*Part I*
People ask me
What happened to our perfect love
Something fractured our unbreakable trust
Healing old wounds can't be rushed
You want it all, but demand too much

Too soon
Your intensity is intoxicating
Free falling
You say that you got me
In a panic I cling to independence
Fighting to let go completely
Asking you to slow down
All you hear is, not now

You could stay
Frustration leads you astray
When I need you the most
With only our future at stake
You choose to escape
Altering fate

All we have is forever
It is only summer
Give me until the New Year
Impatience trigger thoughts of rejection
You give me no time for redirection

Spitefully diverting your attention
One hallows eve with no protection
You say she reminded you of my reflection
Who taught whom the deeper lesson

I would never settle for second best than

The cycle repeats
You plant your seed
In someone other than me
Depriving me the depths of your love
Denying me the capacity
To selflessly surrender
Knowing I could never accept playing 2nd
You assure me that 1st will always be my position
You forget that I am the result of someone's taboo affection

Loyalty should not be in question
My love passes all examination
Mastering the art of divvied affection
I keep my heart under lock & key
Reserving for you the best of me

Forfeit the dream
Fantasizing that you will one day marry me
What will it take for you to see
That your love is no longer free

You plead with urgency for forgiveness
The fidelity you promise
Falls on deafness
You call it pride
I call it self-knowledge
I have already suffered a lifetime of this
God as my witness
I will never occupy space
No longer mine to claim.

*Part II*
Three's company
I remove myself from the equation
My presence only serves as your distraction
Comparison leads to dissatisfaction
It's no longer about you or me
What should have been or could be
I can't handle the emotional weight
No energy to continue the debate
Twice I leave the states
Creating space for your priorities to recalibrate

A year passes & time changes nothing
Except increasing your discontentment
Like a caged panther choosing self-harm
Longing for freedom

Now, you have the capacity to wait
In reality, the choice was already made
Soulmate no longer equates
A shared last name

You won't find me at the altar
My expectations never falter
I reject the sins of my father's father
Breaking generational patterns
I won't accept anything less than
A family tree branching from you & me

In life there is no guarantee
Every action causes an equal reaction
I grow into my womanhood
Wondering if you fully appreciate
What I'm willing to give away

Just to force you to surrender the chase
Finally stick & stay

A less complicated love wins the day
I walk down the aisle in vintage silver lace
Despite the nuptials
Hope never fades
No matter what I do
The bond won't break
Can I finally accept that mistakes were made?

*Part III*

We both explore relationships
Vowing to remain insignificant
Nothing & no one comes between us
With an unspoken agreement
To avoid lasting consequences
That's why you exercising free will
Feels more like the ultimate betrayal

On the topic of trust
I wonder if that is how it hits
When first fruits are given to your stand in
Was it something you should have agreed with
Since we share everything both small & significant
No secrets between us exist
Yet, denying you something so intimate
Makes me the first in violation

Do you feel entitled
To be my one & only love
Believing we would share the big firsts
Reserving homes, marriage & births
Yes, you cut me deep
But I bleed you first
You expect the world from me
When the tables are turned
I give you wings

So many years since our paths first split
You're still in limbo
Not ready to commit
You ask for advice
Should you make it official

You are having doubts
About increasing offspring
We always dreamed of having a team
I give you my unconditional blessing

Affirming your situation
Won't improve unless you're all in
Hindsight changes nothing
Now that I am suddenly free again

My hand comes with the same stipulation
Soulmate, put a ring on it & play your position
Do it for your seeds who deserve
Your loyalty without competition

You say I never loved you the same
The depth & breadth of my love in your soul
Can never change, be erased or replaced
The truth is I love you more than I love myself
Enough to give love away
There is no force more powerful than free will
To make you forget destiny's name

What feels like an outcome undesired
Could in reality be what is needed to transpire
No growth required
You are wanted as is
Given time you may learn
To love the one you're with.

*Commitment*

What part did you miss
The gold band & sparkling drip
The part where I walk down the aisle draped in lace
Or the vows I make, taking his last name
Surrounded by lavender roses on a crisp spring day

Suddenly, I have your full attention
Coming at me with all these hostile questions
Out of all the suitors that have come & left
Why him
What makes him so different

See beloved, it is the follow through
That set him apart
He showed me
When a man is ready
He doesn't just wine & dine
Showering me in flowers & gifts
Taking me on expensive weekend trips

He doesn't run hot & cold
Demanding every day
Then disappearing without a call
He keeps every date never missing a beat
He remembers birthdays
Making sure to be present for all the important things

A man's love is self-evident
More than words of intent
Actions have significance
Behavior is the true revealer
The heart can be fickle
We fall in love with an idea

Some story of happily ever after
Not knowing how to make fantasies a reality

Husband material makes promises that he keeps
Never just the bare minimum
He goes the extra mile asking for my hand
Not backing down from any demand
He slowly builds confidence
While checking off all my lists
He doesn't rush to take up residence
Claiming all my wifely benefits
He respects my space & time
See his mama raised him right

The truth is we choose our own destinies
Through hard work & consistent effort
In our willingness to put aside selfish tendencies
To serve our loved one's needs
True love is an open window slowly closing
When you take an eternity to make a decision
The choice may no longer be an option

One man's distant future
Is another man's priceless treasure today
The man with a heart of gratitude to receive
In life is given everything
The man who doesn't waste time
With divine blessings
Gets down on his knees
Choosing to begin forever today with a ring

Truth is, I didn't know
That his love would be different
I asked the universe to reveal his true intentions

Through unfaltering loyalty
Genuine character, reliability & consistent effort
His commitment proves to be the difference.

*Missing You*
Today, like every day
Since last we spoke
Laughed & joked
For hours on the phone

I miss your smile
The smell of tobacco smoke
Lingering in my clothes
Days after you've gone

Missing your lemonade
Too sweet from sugar
The peach & plum cobbler
You baked for me special

Missing your wisdom
Advice always on point
The acceptance you shown me
Without thinking twice

I know you're still with me
I wish I could feel your hand
Wrapped around mine
Since life began

I miss you daddy
Although I understand
You walk among the saints
Grandma, Grandpa, Auntie & your love
Mary Anne

I'm thankful I got to hold your hand
On your last earthly night

To pray over you, talk with you
Assure you that we'd be all right

I still wake up worried
Wondering why you haven't called
Only to remember with bittersweet sadness
That you've gone home to be with the Lord.
*-Rest in power daddy*

*Ode To The Beautiful One*
The sky turned dark hues
Of purples & blues
Black clouds morphed in a spiral
Between night & day
When the earth trembled & shook
Releasing you
From your princely rule
Back to the One
Who lent you to us
For such a short reign

You lived
In a silhouette of Minnesota cool
With your soul pointed to true north
Your heart pumped indigo blood
Born from the movement
In the spirit of love

Unapologetically Black
Your life was a testament to freedom
Demonstrating that a name
Was not chattel
To be bartered & owned
You taught us
To bow down to no one

Beyond musician
Your sound was a spirit vision
To partake in the experience
Was to glimpse
Into other planes of existence
Every note transcended
You captivated

The ears of royalty
Made the nobodies feel
Like they were worthy of being

One of the most beautiful ones
Your mind spoke in melodies
Your body became the instrument
As you scored the music for this thing called life
Life-force you gave
The love we made
Was timeless

There is not a word to define you
Able to contain your complexity
Describe your genius
Put your music in a box
Still incapable of believing
You departed from us

The first night you ascended
The world was transformed
Every light turned purple in your honor
Your sound circled the globe
While people took to the streets
In an epic celebration of your magnificence

Moving to your music in tandem
Dancing in purple rain
Tantric euphoria triumphed the mourning
Until the second day
When the planet awoke
Wondering if it was all a dream

Your sound

Forever etched in the collective mind
Opens the third eye
While your spirit rides an eternal high
Satisfying hungry souls
With purple guitar strings
Played to a chorus
Of angels & piano keys

Dearly Beloved,
As we say goodbye to a life
Too vibrant for this world
Too abounding in light
Beautiful One
Now become one
With the divine.
*-Rest in power Prince*

*Time*
Once again I see
That we are on different wavelengths
I'm going
Your coming
Circling each other
Unable to sync
Our timing
Has always been off a beat
A second too short
A moment too long

Inverted reality
Walking the same timeline
At different points
In reverse
Sharing a life in tandem
What will it finally take to align
Freeze time
Stand still
Rewind

We meet me in the middle
You say, time will tell
What's meant to be will be
Give it time
All I've given you is mine
All you've taken is a lifetime
I am finally ready to reclaim my time.

## *Mask Off*

Once we were young
Children dreaming of freedom
Not knowing there is nothing more freeing
Than having your whole life undetermined

Our hearts open
We explore innocent love
In the absence of titles & meaning
A wild frontier to conquer
Each new height leaves us wanting to climb higher

Actions lead to reactions
Before the path is chosen
Destination set forth with intention
A simple detour alters your direction

Your seeds bloom
Giving your life beautiful meaning
Guiding you from one selfless decision to the next
Making each progression easier than the last

Just as life blossoms with a purpose
So do the flowers provide themselves fruit
That grow their own seed to sow
Independent of us

Temporal as the blowing wind
So too will life's seasons change
Burdens once all consuming
Begin to ease until released
Returning to you the freedom
Long missed & almost forgotten

Make no mistake life is far from lived
This isn't how the story ends
No, this is just where the plot twists
Turn the page to begin the next chapter

Complacency isn't the same as destiny
The mask you wear isn't your true face
Underneath the mundane you are suffocating
While comfortable familiarity attempts to seal your fate

Be the change
Not the excuse to remain
Have you forgotten how to think creatively
Set independent goals & manifest into reality
You are an artist
Allow your heart to feel renewed
Your mind to dream anew
This is your season to discover you.

## *Manifesting*

There's a difference between happiness & appreciation
You can be both thankful for the blessings
While knowing that this ain't it
The life you've accepted
Is only a fraction of your potential

Manifest your dreams
When are you going to take that leap
Step away from the false security
Of whatever zone that is
You are passing as comfort

You've been drowning in depression
You deserve so much more
Love that's genuine
Real passion, true fulfillment
You only have one life
Let's live it

I believe in giving you space
No pressure, you choose
The only limit is you
When you're ready to be free
I'm here for it
Together we'll manifest dreams into reality.

*Destiny*

Everything on my mind & in my heart
Has already been written & said
I made my peace
With paper & pen

No sense in resurrecting
What is already dead
It is time to evolve
Move forward my friend

You said that you've built
A life filled with love you adore
Yet, in your heart
There is room for more

Let's lean into that notion
Begin to explore
Just like you, I long to restore
A soul fulfilled that desires no more

The only time my restless mind
Experiences peace
Is when I am wrapped in the warmth
Of your company

Do you ever find yourself
Staring at the sky
Watching the clouds shapeshift
As they slowly drift by

Wondering why
The universe
Leaves a revolving door

Spinning between you & I

The globe I traverse
Only to find
Myself right back here
Walking through your door one more time

It is obvious to me
That we are destiny unrealized
The prospect excites my spirit
Knowing the final chapter has yet to be written

The stars continually align
To keep our love in sight
I see no further reason
To deny a purposeful life

All I want is to take your hand again
Give in fully to the whirlwind
Allow the universe to take us for a spin
Letting go control of navigation

Love will lead us
To where we are destined
I no longer accept a life lived with any less than
The true love of my soulmate & best friend.

*Loc'd In Love*

Loc'd not bound
Curly coils fall towards the ground
Hips sway to the beat
Locs grooving with me
Twisting, turning
Bouncing, swirling
My locs come alive

Knotty roots
My locs pay tribute
To ancient routes
Flowing like the Nile River
From tropic waters
Through Nubian dunes
Past jungle ruins
To empty into fertile basins
Fanning like fingers branching
Stretching to feed the Mediterranean Sea

My locs hold herstory
The chapters written in loops & twists
Folding, keeping the secrets
Hidden in the pages of my life
Curling script handwritten
Rolled into paper scrolls
Whispers of poetry
Legendary battles fought
Wars overcome with love
Passionate twisted fantasy

Read my palm rolls
Explore the text-ures with me
Inhale natural aromatherapy

Scented in lavender & honey
My loc's softness caress your face
Lulling you to sink deep into slumber
Dreaming of sipping nectar in the garden
Surrounded by the locs of your Nubian Queen.

*Self Love*
Dear Self,
You are made of pure magic
You grew with me through
Four decades of life
Taking me to breathtaking places
Tender moments & amazing experiences

You walked me down the aisle
Carried me through so many trials
You gave lifeforce to my womb
Birthed a perfectly-made new human

You strengthened my son
With your nourishing serum
Kept up with life's increasing demands
Winning every battle, restoring me to health

Through aches & pains
Abuse & neglect
In so many evolutions
You never quit giving your energy

For all your dips & curves
Scars & stretch marks
I am forever in awe
Of your beautifully flawed perfection
With gratitude,
I love you.

*Shadow Work*

I want to hold you
Caress the back of your head
Massage the tension from your neck
In warmth surround you
My legs & arms around you
Make love to your heart
Gift you pure energy
Until your mind resets
Releasing your body of stress
Wellness restored
All the way to the core
But I can't
This is your journey
Your inner work, your history
You are not a torn garment for me to mend
My weekend warrior DIY project
My inner garden to tend
All I can do is love you
By definition give you space & time
Support your evolution
Make room for the work of the divine
Your transformation will come alive
When you delve into healing inside.

# POETIC ENTICEMENT
*Poems on a journey of the heart.*

*Feature*

You are my soul's teacher
There is no book I write
About my world
Without you in it

You are the feature
Of life's important lessons
Joy & heartbreak since we met
Jewels in my treasure chest

You depart wisdom nuggets
Each time your words flow
My ear eagerly receives
Your generous blessings

My visions of the future
Present obsession
Memories of the past
You are the central figure

Muse, I refuse to omit
Nor edit the divine importance
Every day since
Our pathways intersected

The whole world can loop
Dreaming on repeat
You are my inception
Anchoring me to reality

One of us running towards
The other backpedaling
Until we swap in the middle

Tenet's our love story

While they're stuck in the Matrix
We swallow the red pill
Together battling false agents
Wielding katanas in our black Ray-Bans & leather

It's us & them
No two souls more destined
In the whole world
To traverse this journey
Until the very end
This is our story.

### *The One*

Every love I allow is doomed to disappoint
The closer they come to my star burning bright
The harder they fight to extinguish its light

I'm still waiting for the one who anticipates my every move
With just one look knows when to be patient & when to push
Who makes my soul his study & my heart his muse
Who travels the universe to find me without leaving the room

I'm still waiting for the one who balances my need
With my desire to be free
Who answers my question without either having to speak
Who is unafraid to burn brightly with the light in me he seeks

I'm still waiting for the one who gives
As much energy as he receives
Who whispers to my soul in the ancient dialect of poetry
Who understands that true love is a rare gift
Yet gives his heart freely
I'm still waiting for you to return to me.

*Fire & Ice*
I fantasize
About you & me
Slowly, loving
Every touch
Softly exploring
Both familiar & new
Butterflies flutter
Deep inside
Tickling the tension
So close to relief
We can barely breathe

The sensation of we
Be-coming
Something more
Flames
Raging in me
Longing to be smoldered
By the cool in you
As steam curls
Off the passion
That we create

Kinetically drawn
Together forever
Creating life
From nothingness
Fire & Ice
I imagine our love
Evaporating in an excruciatingly slow
Blissful death
Til nothing is left.

*Power Struggle*
I see you
All of it I want to consume
With a surge of desire
To take & be taken
Battle & make love
Pulling & squeezing
Choking & stroking
Tasting & drinking
Every inch of flesh
That restrains the beast
Ripping & clawing to release
The truth of our nature

Individually we are one
I would use every ounce of energy in me
To see every pound of tension
Within you undone
Your roar invokes no fear in me
Tooth & claw only excite
Go ahead & dig into soft skin
Take a bite
Pleasure in pain
Drink the sweet willingness within
To feed & satiate
I crave to hear the deep rumble of satisfaction
Once you've had your fill

The haze clears & calm takes over
Your eyelids lower
Breathing deepens
Into a steady rhythm
For just a moment
The battle is won

A time to love & be healed
Your walls tremble & shake
Threatening to come tumbling down
A fleeting moment, then it's gone
Back to square one.

*Cocoa Brown*

Memories of you got my panties steaming
Chocolate love still got me feigning
Hungry for your type of craving
Daydreaming
All the ways you keep me begging

I'm drankin
My fingers already misbehaving
Reminiscing
Your lips soft tease
My thighs squeeze
Smooth shaved skin
Vibrations increase
To match my intensity

Chocolate lover
Your love is fire
Melting my walls of desire
Until I plead for release
You finally set my body & soul at ease

Sigh of relief
I laugh
Amazed by how well you still know me
Reading my mind you give me
Exactly what I need
Light one & watch the smoke curl
Higher & higher
Entranced in the rhythm of our heartbeat
We lay as it dances along the ceiling
Captivated by love's energy.

*Distant Dreams*
Echoes of your love
Haunt me in the night
Visions of another time
Born from distant memory
Longing to make anew
Your spirit sees right through
The open door of my mind
You delve deep into the welcome in my eyes
Unraveling the layers of taboo
Until you reach the girl
You once knew

We linger in the warm embrace
Of a sweetness that never fades
By memory fingers gently trace
The curving smile of a face
Time stands still here
Precious seconds disappear
Our souls softly whisper
Without ears we hear
Every unspoken word
Saved for the right moment
We exist with no regret
Innocently, we are free
As the first day we met

I slowly emerge from the haze of deep sleep
My soul clinging to what it cannot keep
When night falls I willingly surrender
To the beckoning call of slumber
Sinking slowly into bittersweet darkness
I think of you as my soul searches
Leaving the window of time open

In comes the familiar breeze of words never spoken
I eagerly welcome your memory to find me
Full of longing
With endless, relentless desire
I welcome your love's haunting.

*Irie*
Your fingers
Linger
Over me
Gently
Brushing every inch
From head to feet

Exploring
Adoring
Words so sweet
Whispered in ears
Lips brushing
Against
Lobes tenderly

Thick locs
Tickle
In between
Soft knees
Quivering
Delivering
Your perfect
Ecstasy

Intertwined
Legs in arms
So divine
Ancient drumming
Keeping time

Simmering heat
Ignites coals of love
So deep

You penetrate
To the very heart of me

Hypnotized
Eye to eye
Your almonds & mine
Passionate kisses
We continue to climb

Yearning
Burning
Molten lava churning within
Digging nails into skin
Grabbing, squeezing
Lace & satin

Sweat glistening
Smooth chocolate
Muscles contracting
Harder & harder
Approaching ascension

Moaning
Groaning
My name
Overflows your lips
Your love explodes
Into fertile rivers
Washing out into the open sea

Exhale tension
Inhale sweet perfume
Your embrace
Gives thanks

For love
Found new
Stay Irie
InI remain with you.

## *Bless Up*

Today you risked it all
Texting wasn't enough
So I answered the call
Jonesing for sapiophilic therapy
Craving spoken word
You enter willingly through the portal
To love's parallel universe

Allow me
To fulfill your need
Speak life into your world
Inhale beauty
Exhale intellect
So satisfying
My poetry is verbalized light
Yet, you achingly realize
It is also your secret demise

Words
There will never be enough of yours
I could hear them all & never bore
Feigning for more
Your mind is magical
You compose the melody
Stringing notes into a heartbeat
Life hangs on every syllable

This is a day to celebrate
I hate to see you in pain
Is reality not meeting
The high standards of your dreams
You see wasted time & give in to frustration
I see hard work & goals manifested

Bless Up
You put in the effort
Next is your reward
You have something magical
A gift that sets you apart
The world sees
A star is born

Your music, your art
Speak of passion & pain
There is so much soul in the songs you sing
Keep fighting, believing, creating
Praise Jah for each victory
Roll a tree let's elevate
Breathe with me & meditate

Think back to that humble room with only a bed
How far you've come
From the toilet under the showerhead
No longer a moody yute
Dressed in head to toe black
Locs tucked under a derby hat

Sleepless winter nights
Making love to stay warm
Unplugged, practicing electric strums
Til your fingers cramp up
Let me massage your hands
With love restore
Here comes your 2nd wind
Ready for more

Now open your eyes & see

You are living your dream
Your babies, your pride, your legacy
The most precious gifts of life
Timeless music to pass down
Through generations
Living in song
The struggle goes on
Strum your guitar
All the way to freedom.

*Conception*
The memory of his love floods my dreams all night
The delicate touch of limber fingers
Strumming notes down the curve of my spine
His soft kisses following their lead
Sending shivers all over me

I vividly relive the fullness of him
Inside my dark chamber
Warming me with pure energy
Bringing my womb to life with his light

I lay back & watch
His smooth amber undertone melanin
Against my honey dipped feet
As painted toes press
Into the firmness of his chest
Wavy lines of sweat trickling
Past two delectable chocolate drops
Down the groove of striations
Pooling in his navel
Vibrating with his abdomen slowly flexing

A vein pulses through a loc covered forehead
Almond eyes so intensely focused on his mission
I dare not disturb the maestro
While he composes his exquisite harmony
I can almost feel his electric guitar reverberating
My eyes study his movements as hips dip & wind
Keeping time with the rhythm of our celestial melody

I revel in his athletic ability
He knows just how much to bend & lean
With divine intuition

He targets that sweet spot as he works the middle
I wonder where he's hidden
The secret map of my body's inner workings
Only he & the creator know so intimately

His star shines with such intensity
He takes command of the darkness
With blinding energy
While the universe pauses
In silent admiration
The angels hover to stare
This is his world going supernova
I'm just grateful to be here

I delight in his natural beauty
Leaving my body to circle behind
Marveling at broad shoulders
Gazing down the V of his spine
To the dip in his hip
Tensing in & out, out & in
A spectator with a bird's eye view
I appreciate his entirety
Watching our love on the big screen
Applauding the effort in 360 degrees

He gently whispers to me,
*Don't move, keep it right here*
Signaling the time has finally come
To re-enter my body
I obediently follow his command
So caught up in watching him loving me
I forget to feel

Suddenly the emotions come flooding in

Overwhelming my senses
My body trembles & shakes
*Yes*, he moans, *give it to me*
His low whispers sending me to ecstasy
Sweet waters overflow as the dam bursts
Through walls of built up tension
His seed comes rushing in
Replenishing the empty void of his creation

Conception
Felt simultaneously
He lays against me
Soft locs tickle my face
Heat radiating from his skin burns against mine
Absorbing the waning quakes of muscles gradually relaxing
He whispers in his smooth tenor
A melody into my ear
Singing a truth that we both can't deny
*You are mine, forever*

I reach out, finally allowed to touch him
Wrapping spent arms & legs around him
I kiss him as I look into his eyes
Swallowing all the passion that's left inside
Our thoughts intermingle
Caught up in the whirlwind
Making silent promises
To never give it away & always remain
I feel the glow of fullness wash over me
From the satisfaction of so much of him
Alive in me
Sowed seeds inside fertile soil
Our lips & hips joined together
Our tongues dance & twirl to love's melody

I hum a simple word of gratitude, yes.

## *Time Traveling*

As I soak my aching body
Fully submerged in a heated tub of eucalyptus salts
Soft golden brown locs make winding paths
Trickling water against caramel skin

Miles wails a blue trumpet jazzy noir
Steam curls dance a slow wind to the ceiling
Escaping from a cracked window
Opened just enough to let the sound of rain in

I relax my mind opening the door for me to write
Paper filled with penned musings
Fall to the damp tiled floor
I wander through dimensions in time
Seeking without searching I explore

I recognize something familiar
When I see you on the other side
Like when you see the welcoming smile of your kin
After a long journey abroad

How the heavy burden of tiredness is lifted
When you finally take your exit
From the winding highways
You've driven all through the night

Embers glow in your eyes with promise
The wall of ice that encircles you
Sweats under the pressure of the heat contained within
If given just the right reason to ignite
They may come crashing down

Enticed, I saunter through the door named desire

To enter your world
Existing within your circle
Close enough to watch sweat trickle down your neck

I sense the hairs of your skin stand as I draw close
I feel the slow steady beat of your flickering pulse
Acutely aware of my electrical presence
The cipher completes as I lean into you.

*Giving Me Life*
He's so good
So good to me
He treats me right
Just like a Queen
Caters to my wants
He's all I need

He's so good
All through the night
His love is strong
He gives me life
His good lovin
Is right on time

He's so good
When I'm low
He lifts me high
Til my smile glows
He holds the recipe
That feeds my soul
Love of my life.

## *Him*

I need him
Like the night needs sleep
Like fresh cotton sheets
Floating on a warm summer breeze
Cool to the touch yet soft underneath
I need him to want me

I want him
With a bottomless desire
With an all consuming fire
That slowly marches forward
Taking over my wilderness never yielding
Rearranging the landscape to breathe again
I want him to love me

I love him
Deeper than the Song of Solomon
Deeper than ancient royalty in the bloodline
I am your queen wearing nothing but your crown on
It's poetic how we love in the garden
With biblical passion seeds are planted
We create legacies or battle plans
I love him more than love's conception.

### *All Of You*

I want it all
Every last inch
Give me the good, the bad, & the ugly truth

I want your whole heart
I'm not afraid of the dark
The murky confusion
The anger, the heat

I can stomach your raw point of view
Take your passion, your unease & your blues
Your love & your black rage
Your dry humor & grief

You're so beautifully complex
It's uncomplicated to me
I want it all, so don't bother hiding from me
Your skeletons, dirty laundry, your quirks & OCD

Let go of the notion
That I won't accept anything less than
Your version of perfection
I prefer the real, so come as you are

That's how it has always been
From the day we first met, & every day since
You accept all of me
The beautifully, complicated, wild
Restless, passionate, everchanging
Evolutions of me

Give me my due
I deserve all of you

The way you receive all of me & choose love
I choose you.

*You Are Love*
Since day one
Your tall stature
Bigger than life
Bending low through the door
To enter my world
You tower over me

You are love
Smooth buttery skin
That glows golden within
The soft wave in your fade
The shy curve of your grin
Your soul shines genuine

You are love
I feel your subtle attention
Watching me walk through the corridors
Come around the corner
I find you standing there
Offering the comfort of your arms

You are love
There's a stillness in you
A calm confident force
So sure of life
So sure of love
So sure of us

You are love
Complicated peace
Brilliant normalcy
Intentional spontaneity
Steadfast unpredictability

Loyal freedom
My beginning to new endings
When you exist, there is a me

You are love
With the energy to create
You bring ideas to life
You solve the impossible
You understand the unfathomable
You give hope to the lost cause
You heal the incurable
Your love is the light in the void

You are love
You are my reason
To breathe
To dream
To smile
To desire
To be

There is no world without you
No life worth living
No point existing
No love without you
You are my everything
You are my love
You are worthy
You are valued
You are wanted
You are irreplaceable
You are necessary
You are loved.

*An Introduction*
I don't know you
But I see you
I've never touched you
Yet I feel you
I want more
Open the door

Not to possess, but to experience
A simple, savage introduction
Raw induction into the world of your creation
I welcome your imagination
Unlock the gate to your mind's inner kingdom

Lose track of time as we explore
Permit me to roam your halls
Contemplate battle paintings on the walls
Blow the dust off records in your collection
Pull up a chair to listen
Enter the throne room
Study your strategy
Browse your library, read your thesis

See I'm feelin a certain way about you
Vibe with me for a moment
I have words to speak true
Since your lips first parted time
Spilt thoughts into verses & rhymes
Revealing your mind

I cannot shake this feeling
Growing inside my being
Where dark waters give life

Even deeper still
My carnal hunger awakens
Warming me with desire
Rousing my inner beast
But it's not weakness beckoning
You're not my prey, you are a siren

Your song draws me to my doom
Calling me towards you
Tempting me to ignore
The jagged rocks along shore
Your melody hypnotizes
Threatens to capsize me
Your energy clings like dampness
Drowning me in my sleep
A dense fog seeping into everything
You offer no hope for escape

I submerge to study you
Drifting all the way to the core
Eyes closed listening
To your spoken word laid against drumlines
Base reverberates as you rhyme
You speak of chains being broken
Visions of shackles open

I watch your lips move with fervor
Through clenched jaw releasing lyrical murder
I smile in amusement
As your fury destroys the competition
Your words tear limb from limb
Only to build them slowly back again
Seeking atonement
You gradually win their confidence

Give them hope for reconciliation

Then you flip a switch
Obliterate the whole building
Killing every soul within
Collateral damage, you laugh as you walk away
It's all a game of strategy you play
A mental escape from the mundane

I hear you
What you say & what you omit
Your longings & desires
Loyalty & honor
Visions of people doing better
A life beyond limits
The depths of your heart
Mourn their wasted potential

How can we collectively win
Still blind to the competition
You are a warrior without a battlefield
Facing an invisible army
Instead of war you rage
Captive energy bursting your veins
Until nothing remains

Like a reflection in a mirror
I see myself in you
In the deep recesses of your mind
There's an invitation to freedom
To unleash the primal being
Leaving behind all that is civilized.

*Tantric*
Love Antidote
The best I ever had
Is love I have yet to make
Love unrealized, yet metaphysically explored

This lover & me
Exposing our truest forms
Hearts in unison
Divine timing
Traversing open minds

This lover in me
Teaching me the meaning of intimacy
Caressing my soul
Reaching the depths hidden beneath
Making love to my inner being

His will takes over my own
I crave his dominance
Whatever he wishes is my command
Where he leads I long to follow

My heart beats in rhythm with his
His air breathes within my lungs
Our tantric energy is one
A lifetime has passed & we've just begun.

*Breathless*
How do you do this
Each time you enter
Sucking the air right from the room
Your presence
Giving me tunnel vision
You inhale the breath from inside my lungs
Everything blurs
Now there's just us
Fade to black

Magnetic
You consume space
Drawing me to you
Leaving no oxygen
Suffocating to exist independently
Without you in me
You live in my skin
Controlling my fear
No inhibitions
I can't help myself

You leave me breathless
Restless
Tossing & turning
Unable to sleep
Staring at the ceiling
Questioning life's meaning
You look at me with such intensity
You see through my defenses
Honest as a newborn
Taking my first breath in
Wondering who I am
Where I wanna be

My love is freedom
Go ahead breathe
Spread your magnificent wings
There's no cage with us
Take to the sky
What kind of souls are we
If not able to fly
When in need return to me
There's no distance too far
To lose sight of where love resides.

*Love & Light*
It's Pisces season
I dream of lost souls
Swimming up the cosmic stream toward home

Consciousness
I feel you moving near
Your breath warms the nape of my neck
I turn too quickly to find you've disappeared

This time of year
It's such a struggle
To remain in the present
When perpetually haunted by your presence

An idea begins to take form
A seed watered
Starts to unfurl
Revealing its secrets to my mind

I could send something
To traverse the space between us
A gift of love & light
Would arrive just in time

I pour my soul
Into tangible form
Working my hands
Seeing with eyes closed

Envisioning my pure energy
Transferring into the mold
I whisper to it our stories
Tales lived so long ago

Out flies tissue paper & tape
Crinkle fill & string
Folded, tucked & wrapped
The gift is ready for sending

I feel both exhausted & energized
Like when you finally arrive
After such a long drive
A slow welcome kiss
From being longed for & missed
The sweat covered glow after climax
A blissful feeling of emptiness

I imagine as I drift
My gift reaching its destiny
Something crafted by my hands
Blessing your skin

Healing vibrations
Allowing you to relax your mind
To release all that is pent up since the last time
I held you wrapped in calm

Feeling your heart beat slow into a steady rhythm
There's peace in stillness
Each breath a millennia
Allowing release of the heavy burden of grief

Breathe out
A moment of nothingness
Death in one beat
Leading to rebirth in the next

Breathe in
I open my depths
To blow this fertile seed
Bursting with life into the wind
It carries inside it a promise with intention

That when you receive this blessing
It will take root deep within you
Sprouting ideas like branches
Limbs of ingenuity reaching upward

Budding with inspiration
Growing until your spirit breaks through
Into your fruitful season
To bloom with love & light.

*Snippet*
Our story
Which chapter we on
Future, past or present
The cypher completes
360 degrees
Whenever we meet

I bet you never knew
Somethin so soft
Could get so hot
Somethin so hot
Could feel so moist
Somethin so moist
Would hug you so tight
Somethin so tight
Could be so right
Somethin so right
Would be yours for life.

*Vow*

You, who have given everything
Just to be with me
All that you were
All that you knew
Putting me before everyone
To embrace the unknown together
You, who calms me
Faces the trials
Every tribulation
With honor & integrity
You, who honored me
Who took me as your wife
Bravely, trusting with mighty faith
Beautiful grace
You are my rock
My anchor
The foundation of all I create
You are my lighthouse
Guiding me home in the night
Guardian of peace
Warrior for Christ
In all that I do
You stand by me
In all that I am
You accept me
You are all that I want
Everything I need
You make life easy
Because you are my blessing
My reason for being
You are the one
The only one for me.

*Love*
Beauty
In your eyes
Hypnotizes me
Overcome by
Emotion
My soul
Opens the door
Allows
You in
Giving way
To arousal
My cup
Filling
To the brim
Your spell
Your smell
I dwell
In your
Presence
Overflowing
Enjoying
The essence
Of you
Never leaving me
Never needing me
Slowly becoming
The air
I breathe
Internally
Your lure
So sure
I am
Of true

Of love
Of you.

*Not Tonight*
Amaze
Trailblaze
Set the stage
Turn a page
Not tonight

Run
Lift
Kick ass
Take names
Not tonight

Dress
Dance
Pop bottles
Turn up
Not tonight

Meditate
Create
Innovate
Take a leap of faith

Maybe tomorrow
I'll do, say, try all those things
Tonight, I'll just be present with you.

## *Vibrations*

There's vibrational energy between us
Undeniable even though we just met
I feel like I've known you forever
I wonder if we are meant to explore this further

So familiar when you stand close to me
I lose all ability
To concentrate on the task at hand
Your frequency makes all my lil hairs stand on end

I'm acutely aware of your presence
The curve of thick lips smiling gentlemanly
I can almost feel their softness
Is that destiny I hear calling

Time stands still when you're next to me
The warmth of your breath
Tickles the back of my neck
I turn to you slowly

You move closer still closing the space between us
*Is something wrong,* you ask me
Reading conflicting emotions in my eyes
From you I cannot hide

*Do you feel that energy?*
I reply by placing my hand on your chest
You tremble with anticipation at my slightest touch
Heartbeats quicken from the transfer of heat between us

I raise my eyes to find
Yours glistening down at mine
You swiftly lean in to kiss me

With such gentle determination sparks fly

I savor the flavor
Of your lips against mine
Tasting your essence
With my tongue's tip

When I take a little bite
Some primal instinct in you ignites
Grabbing a handful of me
You lift my leg above your thigh

Pressing into me
I feel excitement swell
Promising something amazing
Mind-blowing, mystical

We hear voices in the next room
Snapping us back to reality
Wait a minute, I say breaking free
Don't you have somewhere to be?

You move away, then hesitate
Minds racing between alternate universes
One life as it is: mundane, uncomplicated
The other vibrating higher with us together

I can see your internal battle waging
Questioning our chance meeting
You need to go
You long to stay

I don't even know your name
Who are you, where did you come from?

All I know is that your someone's son
Smooth bald head, caramel complexion

Ready to make my world more interesting
Introduce a deeper intimacy
Rewrite my story
By giving love a new beginning

You decide life is too short for regrets
Looking through the windows of my soul
You speak to destiny by telling me,
*I am exactly where I need to be.*

## *Peace*

You have this uncanny way
Of smiling at me
That silences all my anxiety
With quiet confidence
You pacify
Leaving me no other choice but to comply
Your perfect timing
Silences fear
With the precise words
I need to hear
Anger melts
In your calm presence
When you touch me
I instantly forget
The conflict
It's a different peace
When you're with destiny
All I want is your love
Inside of me
Surrounding me
In silent harmony
Reminding me
That there's nothing else for me
Besides your mellow love.

## *Summer Of Love*

Dreaming so sweetly
Heart rhythms beating slow & steady
Hypnotic drifting
You are sinking deeper
Penetrating the abyss
Floating in blackness
Can you feel me near
Melodically whispering in your ear
Singing a love story
So distantly familiar

It is a stormy night in early September
The sky is spinning black & green
We still in these streets
Wishing summer would never cease
The crew's been in the cipher since three
You've dropped home everyone but me
Saving the best for last
I recognize the signal still I pretend to be naive
Driving down empty streets
Wheels splashing against concrete
You turn down 28th Street
The hum of the engine drowned out by a sudden downpour
Water beats down in waves
What a violent storm
Distant thunder rumbles drawing near
Lightning flashes it's electric heat
The sole lamp flickers on my dimly lit street
I reach for the door as you reach behind me
Closing it swiftly before the flood takes me
Tonight there is no escape
You pull me so close
You take my breath away

Your kisses quickly revive me
Now the storm is growing inside
The metallic pounding on the rooftop
Overshadowed by the race of my thundering heartbeat
You bite into me & let your tongue soothe away the searing heat
My painted toes curl along the ceiling
Everything disappears in a whirlwind of bare skin
Your hands
Your mouth
Where do I end & they begin
We are everywhere
Over, under, inside one another
Transported into the eye of the storm it's quiet
Wrapped inside a love cocoon hidden from the chaos
We forget fear
Forget inhibitions
Forget we're still parked out here
Watery headlights pass by
Our love is hidden by steam vapors
Condensation trickles down clouded glass windows
You make it all melt away
You take me to your secret universe
With you
With you
With you
There's only trust
No more them just us
Your love is the cure
You make the pain fade away
This moment is all that remains
There's only us
Breathing as one
Dreaming in unison
Wrapped in each other's warmth

Until the rain stops
Until the dawn breaks
Until tomorrow chases away today.

*Ecstasy*
Your hands expand
Fingers fanned
Taking command
You touch me
Whispering sweet nothings
You oooo me
Thighs tingling
You awww me
Controlling
Moaning
Rolling
Eyes mesmerized
You taste me
Groans escape
Embrace me
Nails digging
Teeth sinking deep
You please
You tease
You bring love to its knees
Then release
You in me
Pure ecstasy.

*Lovers*

Lovers love love
Every part of love
Each breath from first to last love
The sleepless anticipation of new love
The nervous flutter of love unfamiliar
The hope of love's exploration
The passion of love's heated touch
The excitement of love returned
The longing of distant love
The mourning of love lost
The regret of love unrealized
The pain of unreciprocated love

Lovers love love
I willingly give up one love for something more
I vow with a ring as a constant reminder
I sacrifice passion to gain love's purpose
I discover a different type of love
A new season with a new reason to love
The tiniest of loves begin hidden
Growing stronger within
Feeding on love
Until it swells unbearably
Bringing love forth into life
Becoming an endless, bottomless, limitless love

Lovers love love
The instant love felt in the first cry
That calls on queens to act selflessly
In effort to soothe every tear
To commit & hold steadfast in their resolve
To nurture love in the light of the sun
Until love becomes man

Releasing love into the world
Ready to begin love's journey again

Lovers love love
I long to open love's vault
Unleashing love's all consuming emotion
To burn with eternal fire
To want & be desired
Sharing love's secrets
In the darkest innermost chambers
Healing old wounds with light & love

Lovers love love
One day, when beauty is mostly silver & gray
When fine lines smile all over my face
Familiar hands will caress
Familiar lips will tenderly kiss
These eyes will whisper poetry
In love's familiar embrace
This lover will endlessly love & love once more
Soul's quiet, destined, timeless love.

### *Slow Burn*

When you stand so close to me
A slow burn ignites
I look into your eyes
The magnetic force between us
Makes everything rise
Resistance is futile
I extend to the tip of my toes
Just to reach your lips
The nape of your neck tickled by my fingertips
Pulling you down to inhale my scent
Intoxicating as it is
Kiss my soul, slowly

Heat smoldering
When we touch
It's wildfire
Wilderness is overcome by desire
Burning brighter
To consume & be devoured

You strip me to the bone
Then suck what's in the middle
Until toes curl
Wetter still
My fountain bursts
Into a growing tidal wave
Washing over our raging flames
Leaving a trail of steam in its wake
Swim or evaporate
Choose your fate
I calm the raging sea for you
Come what may I got you

Our love transforms into a gentle rain
Washing away scorched earth
Enters our second wave
Simmering down the temperature
Bathe with me in warm tranquil waters
Let my love surround you
Healing your troubles
Soothing what aches
Mind, body & soul
Give it all to me
I'll be loves keeper
With me your secrets are safe

Set your spirit free
Two becoming one
We achieve a stillness
Reaching peace
Minds wide open
Unspoken thoughts
Asked & answered
With just a look
Impossible choices
Destiny makes no mistakes
Shared fates
Patiently
Unchanged
Unchained
Love remains.

## *Whirlwind*

It is a warm & sunny Wednesday
Summer sparkles emerald green against blue sky
Nothing spectacular this afternoon to remember
We are young, in love & happy to be together
You say that we should get something to eat
We begin to leave, then you stop & think
In the driveway you get down on your knees
Smiling up at me with eyes glistening
You present a shimmering diamond & pearl ring
My eyes open wide beginning to sting
I stare down at you in disbelief
Pulling me close you ask, *Will you please marry me?*
I rapidly blink away the stream of tears
Agreeing to be yours without reservation or fear
You lift me in your arms smiling as big as the sun
We laugh & spin around
My feet have yet to touch the ground

I will never forget how it felt
To have my heart swell
With so much joy it overwhelms
With the promise of a future not yet told
Enduring love to have & to hold
Together until our days grow old
For every question, *Will you?*
We answer freely, *I will!*
Today we kiss single goodbye
Committing to the rest of our lives
We vow to stay by one another's side
Abiding in love through happy & trying times
On a random Wednesday in love's endless summer
We became man & wife.

*Day One*
He says,
One night with you & I won't go
Back to my wife
I'll change my whole life
I've wanted your love for the longest time
Please don't let this be another test
I've been waiting for this moment since we met
Just ask me to stay
It'll be like the first day

I say,
Pure love would cure
Your deepest pain
Still I can't be the one
To soothe what aches
I wouldn't let you
Throw it all away
I'd rather remove myself
Than keep you
From doing the right thing

He says,
You couldn't stop me
If you let me have all of you
I promise I won't be able to stay away
I can barely stand the daily facade
Smiling like nothing's wrong
When I'm with you it feels like coming home
No need to pretend
I find myself again
That's why we can't be friends

I try to understand

How one touch can change a man
Obliterate the barriers that barely stand
Give into one's need for a soul that is free
Like coming towards the surface from way down deep
Breaking through to air
That you so desperately need
Do I really expect a man who can finally breathe
To return to the depths of misery
So no, friends we cannot be

He stands so tall
Always towered over me
Tonight he gets down on his knees
To plead he wraps his long arms
All around me
Pulling me close
He says,
When I look into my baby's eyes
I realize how much I'm needed
I'm their whole life
My happiness is the cost
I'm at a daily loss
Trying to be a better man
I deny myself for them
That's why we can't be friends

I look through his eyes
To speak to his soul
I love you
*I love you*
I want you
*I want you*
I need you
*I need you*

You give me life
In darkness,
You are the spark that ignites
My fire warming the coldest of nights
You are my torment burning so bright
I am the moth hypnotized
I cannot fight
The urge to plunge myself into your light
Let your flame consume me
Let it transform the fiber of my being
Leave nothing untouched
My former self burns to ashes & dust

He says,
Consumed by desire
Your love is pure energy
You make me high
I elevate
I vibrate
When we become
I won't survive
I metamorphosize
When we become one
I am undone

I say,
You understand me
You know me
When you speak to me
You whisper poetry
In a secret language
That only my soul comprehends
You hear my inner thoughts
You complete unspoken sentences

Before I ask
You answer life's questions
You keep my secrets
You truly see me
You see who I can be
You see infinite possibilities
You uplift me
You encourage me
You believe in me
You are my missing peace
Your love sets me free
I agree
That is why friends
We
Cannot
Be
Still I want you to stay


He lifts me up
In an embrace that leaves the ground
Completely exposed
Baring our souls to one another
We vibrate love in surround
No words left unspoken
In perfect silence we breathe
Two souls sheathed in comfort
Completely at ease
Sharing a fleeting moment of peace
Eyes closed, minds open we finally see
Truth so real it sets us free
Silently our souls weep


Candlelight flickers
Making shadows dance to silent rhythms

As the moon makes its ascension
Shimmering through mountain valleys
Illuminating our glow
The tide slowly grows
From chocolate peaks
Caramel rivers flow
Into a rising melanin sea
We drift freely
Dreaming, breathing, loving, existing
In a sacred space
It's getting late. . .
We embrace with a goodnight kiss
I say goodbye to my friend
He says, thank you
Grateful for a gift rescinded.

~

Since Day One
You've been there
Loving me thicker than blood
True love is freedom
You finally understand
Love with no limits
Relationships evolve
I learn by letting go
A soulmate I have found.

# RETURN PASSAGE
*Poems of the struggle.*

*Sistah Long Legs*
Hey sistah long legs
I see you making your way
Sunlight glistening
On all that brown skin, shealoe & melanin

G'wan & sashay
Down the promenade
Full lashes under cateye sunglasses
Fenty Uncensored lips parted in a subtle grin
Nonchalance that you've perfected

The sea breeze ruffles your animal print caftan
Chiffon flowing freely belted high above the waist
Floppy hat & bare legs
36 inch goddess box braids
Swaying as you saunter down to the beach

You carry the weight of the world on full hips
But one would never know it
Your confident stride
Has perfected the *not bothered* vibe
So you don't show it

Your brilliant mind
With a master's degree in problem solving
Working on your legacy
While you multitask
Minding your own business, healing & growing

You manifest as you master tasks
Breaking through glass ceilings
Pushing yourself to level up
Who runs the world

You, CEO Boss Chic, all before lunch

The world is your oyster
You work smart so you can play harder
Planning your next global takeover
Pack an overnight bag
It's time to hop a plane & start your bae-cation

You dine at a table set for twelve amongst the vines
Sipping wine as you unwind
Laughing with your girls at the latest tea
Escapades retold of past loves
Shared visions you discuss coming to fruition

Loyal to love, faith & family
In pursuit of dreams
You slay the game #staywinning
You deserve life's finer things
You're so dedicated

I love breaking bread with you
Let me pour a drink for you
In the kitchen working your magic
Skills so heaven sent get mouths watering
Everything you create smells amazing

Mama would be so proud of you
She's smiling down on you
Cheering for every accomplishment
Keep ya fist balled up
Marching forward fulfilling your destiny.

### *Wanderlust*
Nomadic
Always moving around
Spirit stays restless
What am I running from

Wheels up
Engines thrust
Feel the immediate stress relief
Problems dissipate
With the city shrinking
Disappearing beneath me
In a swirl of dust

I wonder if I'll be back again
Forever looking forward
Searching for peace
Manifesting dreams
Setting goals
Making plans

Trust the journey
It's a faith walk
Looking for what feels right
A place to thrive
Catch a vibe
Where spirit comes to life

We are a people stolen
Captive so long
We've forgotten our origin
A tribe of brown kin
Forever wandering the diaspora
Home is wherever we land.

*Azure*

A silver speed train charges down the track effortlessly
Past a blur of golden hills
Neat rows of autumnal colored vines
It's wine country

We pause in sleepy towns with meandering cobblestone roads
Crowded with village shops showcasing windows
Full of freshly baked pâtisseries
The doors open & the smell of buttery flakiness tempt me to disembark
A moment longer & we are off again charging forward

Racing along the Riviera
Ancient vines give way to a gem colored sea
The warm sun kisses our cheeks as we exit
The creaky wooden platform to the street

Strolling toward the water we find an open air market
The pretty scent of blushing peonies
Beckon to our noses to come closer
Galvanized buckets overflow with delicate stems
Showcasing yellow provence blooms
Fluffy soft petals tickle as I stoop to breathe in

A chalk covered sidewalk sign catches the corner of my eye
I saunter over to the next stall to see what treasures I find
A scribbled handwritten note hanging from twine rope reads,
*Savon de Marseille, Olive, Lavande, Lait*
Introducing a table filled with endless rows of pastel colored soaps

We stop at the corner mart for sparkling perrier & warm apple tart
A friendly cashier asks us if she can practice her English
Smiling, she hands us our change & says, *have a lovely day*
Content with shopping we stroll the Promenade des Anglais

Admiring colorful hand painted art depicting scenes
From the River Seine & Champs-Élysées
We sit to read Elle magazine under the shade of a mimosa tree

Curiously eavesdropping on animated conversations
Too dramatic to translate
We spy hairy beachgoers in tiny speedos
Parading past pale breasted dames sunbathing topless
The setting sun warmly greets the azure coast
Casting rays of citron & marmalade
Against a cyan colored horizon
Dotted with white shimmering yachts anchored in the bay.

*Black Star*

For your consideration
Mental stimulation
Thought process
Two of the greatest
Iconic
Hypnotic
The swerve in your tonic
Have mercy
Mercy mercy me
Keep you moving
Keep you on your feet
Back & forth
Four hundred years plus two more
It's a black star
Illuminating the way home
Returning across the passage
One way voyage on the Atlantic
To the Mother City
Welcome home
Lost soul
Black man
The original
Where I belong
Blackness I come from
To blackness I return
I am that I am
An African reborn.

*Quiet Storm*
I jus wanna lay in silence
Let the rain fall
Cleanse our fears
Wash away the violence

As we detox
The earth is weeping
So tired of reaping
This toxic harvest

Our babies are infected with us
We jus keep spreading the sickness
How many black & brown lives must be culled
Until we finally heed the call

Face the writing on the wall
This is a purge & we're the victims
No one left to claim reparations
Lightens the burden on the richest

Put our ish aside of self
Prioritize physical & mental health
Healing the spirit opens doors to wealth
Do the inner work so we can collectively gain

Where are we going if not together
My people deserve so much better
Don't wait for them to send relief
The flood is here & we're just getting wetter
They rather let us drown then share prosperity

Quietly we build don't let them see
Knowledge is power read between the lines

Ownership builds legacy
Now I'm just collecting deeds

I just wanna see my people finally succeed
Take me to my birthright across the sea
To find my peace in a land where I can finally breathe
So my seed can walk in the freedom to pursue his dreams.

*Freedom*

Where can I live without the threat of violence
Where my safety isn't paid for with my silence
Freedom to exist fully in my darkness
Where melanin is just sun-blessed skin
Not the reminder of your original sin

You create systems to keep us in order
Instead of admitting wrong & finding closure
As long as you continually perpetuate the beast
History is stuck on repeat
You will never find your elusive peace
Until reparations are paid
Freeing my people of this legacy.

### *Unapologetic Rhetoric*

Black & Unapologetic
I'm black & unapologetic
You're black & unapologetic
She's black & unapologetic
We're black & unapologetic

When you enter the war room
Bow to the Queen
Assemble the team what's the strategy
We create legacies or battle weapons
I'm the dragon mother bring my war chest

Black & Unapologetic
I'm black & unapologetic
You're black & unapologetic
She's black & unapologetic
We're black & unapologetic

They label us militant
I call us resilient
We keep fighting with fists balled up
Raise them high to the sky
Black Lives Matter the battlecry

Black & Unapologetic
I'm black & unapologetic
You're black & unapologetic
She's black & unapologetic
We're black & unapologetic.

*Police Traumatic Stress Disorder (PTSD)*

Someone's wife & mother, son & father
They killin us, Lord they killin us
Pops had it wrong
The revolution is being live streamed on every TV
Body cams & cell phones tell no lie
I wonder if they cry as they watch us die

An innocent man bled from his chest pumped full of lead
The world watched him die a slow & painful death
With cop gun cocked on his child & woman
No one allowed to try
To preserve black life
While he sputtered drowning
In his innocent blood
Where is the justice

Keep your thoughts & prayers
Since all lives matter
Only black skin gets vigilante justice
Denied The Constitutional right to due process
We die in the street surrounded by blue & red lights
Our last breath is of blood & gun smoke
The only thing missing is the white hood & cloak

Someone's wife & mother, son & father
They killin us, Lord they killin us
What do I tell my seed of this violence & greed
What do I tell my seed, to stand tall or get down on his knees
Do I tell my seed his people were original Kings & Queens
Do I tell my seed now his life means nothing
Lord they killing us
Lord they killing us

I never had money for nice things
I never had hope to dream dreams
Everything we had was borrowed or handed down used
All I knew was brokenness
All I wanted was something new
It's so easy to keep us down
We stay oppressed in our comfort zone
They got they foot on our necks

We medicate to relieve the stress
Now we're addicted & depressed
Sex, liquor, molly, pills
Keep the pain numb- our brains dumb
Church on Sunday, Lord redeem
We sing slave songs

God forgive me, for comfort I nearly sold my soul
Ghosts haunt my sleep
There's no rest, I fear I'll lose control
I stay cutting ties from the past & never looking back
The very brick I buy to build with- the man still holds the check
With borrowed roots there is no foundation to build our wealth
We leave nothing behind for our seeds but unfulfilled dreams

All that I am
Everything I do- it's all for you
To never know these streets or have to hustle to eat
I feed you love & wisdom
So you stay mentally fit, & grow spiritually strong
I gave you life so you can lead, live better than me
Dare I hope that you'll live until old & have your story told
Not shot down by police, blood filling the street
Black mothers get no rest, without justice no peace

Someone's wife & mother, son & father
They killin us, Lord they killin us
What do I tell my seed of this violence & greed
What do I tell my seed
Stand tall or get down on his knees
Do I tell my seed in his blood lives royalty.
*"There can be no justice without peace & there can be no peace without justice."*
-M.L.K. 1967

*Dear All Lives Matter*

They distract us with money, cars & clothes
Turn us into capitalist hoes
We gain things without possessing wealth
Our future is chattel they borrow & sell

It's true they killin us, be we also kill ourselves
They gave us drugs & guns, but who pulled the trigger
How can we turn our pain into rage & demand change
When we still have ourselves to blame?

They let a few of us come up so the rest can hate
We work to serve, they cut that check
We pay to play
Modern day slave
They own the game
We're easy prey
They build the prison, control the courts
Write the law that they enforce
The system is a ball in chain
Time to file for divorce

For that bling you dance & sing
Dribble & swing
The cycle continues stuck on repeat
Our soul has been in bondage
Since our cousins sold us to those ships
Hands above your head, down on your stomach
Feel that pistol whip
Mobilize, march with signs
Try & change their minds
There is no freedom, there is no peace
We are captives of the beast

They got us fighting over black & blue
When all that matters is that green
They own the banks, print the dollar
Hoard all the money & power
When we sleep we dream of cheddar
Wake ready to chase that cream
In this crazy world they rule everything

They assert their power as we struggle to breathe
Still hanging nooses from trees, makes me sick with grief
I don't want my son to catch this illness
Where is the vaccine
To keep us immune from the diseased state of police.

*Blacklight (Revisited)*
A new immigrant once asked me, is it hard to be black?
The question gave me pause
To give an answer I had to first explain,
What it is to be "black"
In this land of freed captivity

I told the immigrant,
Black, as an American construct, has never been free
Black was created as a differentiation
To set apart, redefining a man from less than
It was stolen, forced, sold as chattel & enslaved

Black did not come to this country as a refugee seeking safety
An immigrant in search of new opportunity
It does not share in the pride of the American Dream
For black there is no part of the story
Where the journey ends in refuge, asylum, or peace

Black means for others to expect gratitude
For the gift of a life sentence of false imprisonment & servitude
For every generation that came before & all to follow

Black is to be told, "don't like it go home"
By the same mouth that forced assimilation
While erasing a history & knowledge of civilization

Black is the world pushing down on one's back
While carrying the weight of community needs
With nothing left for self

Black is having to forego dreams
Lumped into a zip code to be gerrymandered & denied representation
Resources for education, health & basic needs

Black is learning how to hustle to eat
Destined to labor & toil for endless capitalist greed

Black is having to say, I can't breathe
With the system's knee on your neck never letting up
Black is vigilante justice swinging from a tree
While their children picnic sipping lemonade enjoying the breeze

Black is to be pushed aside & passed over
Detained, experimented on & exploited
Taxed, fined, censored & denied voting rights
Profiled, stop & frisked, violated & imprisoned

Black is to be shot & killed while surrendering
Under represented, despised & misunderstood
The punch line to a joke the entire country
Shares with the developed world

A stepchild fostered
By the same "parental" authority who inflicted abuse
Black is having one's history omitted
Rewritten so a whitewashed version is taught in schools

We lose & we lose & we lose
But stay #winning
Refusing to be labeled a burden
In a brainwashed mixture of pride & guilt

Yes, it is hard to be black
To suffer loss at the hands
Of those who never express regret
Injured with no reparations

We smile, we pose, we entertain

We hide behind a mask of dignity
Intellectual indifference
Spiritual forgiveness

In blackface minstrelsy we mask the deep hatred
Of history, of self, of our oppression
Ingrained over centuries into the fiber of our being
Becoming more fused to our marrow

With each generation the cycle continues
How can we love our children
Honor our mothers
Embrace patriotism

When the message we receive
The minute we tune in
Log on
Step outside
Is that our color is undesirable, less than

Something to compensate for like a tarnished reputation
A hurdle to overcome, our success is described as "despite of"
Never "because of" our blackness
Our being is reduced to a setback in a five letter word,
Black

We are the perpetual blemish on an otherwise perfect society
A living, breathing contradiction
While others pretend to not see us

Ignored, like we are not worthy of acknowledgement
Avoid us with suspicion
Cross to the other side of the street
How strange others seem

Their behavior betrays their prejudice
Despite what their sign says
Every time they instinctively shift away
Become nervously defensive of their belongings

Karen following us acting in some misguided authority
Because of their home training
Because of some profile
They think black fits the description

Black is to stare in the mirror daily
Trying to change oneself to be less threatening
Less natural, less beautiful, less real

Less authentic, less ethnic, less seemingly militant
Black is to be conditioned to self-hate
The pigment of brown skin & ebony hair
Thick locs, coils & kinks

The curves in all the useful places
The muscles both short & defined, long & lean
That give us the abundant strength
Grace & physical advantage
That makes our existence
Black persistence to be
Black audacity to believe
So threatening
Our very existence exposing the American Lie

We have our own story to tell
Our music is more complex
Our stories contain more depth
Our art has greater dimension

Our ingenuity is more inspired
Our culture is more ancient
Our parables hold more meaning
Our soul food has more seasoning
Our leadership has more compassion
Our communities are more inclusive

We redefine us, flip the script
Blackity Black Black
Rooting for everyone black becomes the anthem
The struggle is real, but no longer defines us
It unites us
We speak for ourselves
Collective living, breathing, oxymoron
We are blacklight
That illuminates what is hidden in plain sight
We expose the ugly truth disguised in their justification
With every achievement we make
Every record we break,
Every triumphant success
We blackout the dark, bitter, nonsensical, insecurity
Behind their biased behavior
Every time we,
The last in line, the bottom, the least of all, WIN
It is a monumental exclamation

We refuse to succumb to the falsity that we are any less than
We reject the notion that we are a menace to be feared & controlled
The only thing to fear is reality itself
When they finally wake up to understand
That despite all the lies they were taught to believe
We are everything they thought we could not be
We are more than
We are able

We always find a way
We are still here
We, the beaten, but not broken
The pillaged, but not diminished
The weary, but not depleted
The shadowed, but luminescent
The caricatured, but still true
We are blacklight & we're here to stay.

*The Morning After*
We deny ourselves
The very thing that makes us feel alive
We don't ask why
We don't even try
We are hopelessly unfulfilled
Desperately in denial
Tirelessly spinning the web of deceit
Generation after generation stuck on repeat

We go through our days & nights
Living their shallow version of a life
Never willing to realize
The time rapidly passing by
We pretend to be unaware
Struggling without a care
We don't even dare to compare our misery
To the people we perceive to live carefree
We don't know what it feels like,
What it looks like, what it smells like,
What it tastes like
To walk free in our happiness
Fulfilling destiny

We keep swallowing the pill
Numbing our will
Surrendering our vigor
To float in the haze that is consciousness
Suppressing the urge for independence
We have too much yet still want
Feel so little we lose empathy
Complain & complain, but never dare to change
We are tired, washed up, lame versions of our true selves
We chase after material wealth

Hoping for egotistical fame
We repress regret to forget so we can maintain the same
Everyone plays the game

Will we ever be free
To be needed & to accept need
To breathe in the wind of our own decisions
When will we let go & learn to love
When will we have had enough lies
Finally take charge of our lives
Maybe we'll open our eyes tonight
Awake to give our long slumber certain death
Freeing our minds to receive the light.

## *The Beast*

Don't wake the captive beast
It gently purrs as it sleeps
Breathing in long steady draws
Razor sharp claws rest within massive paws
Quietly humming is the heart of a giant
Its mighty chest heaves & rises

Please do not wake this beast
Seemingly peaceful while asleep
There is something deeply troubled beneath
Its calm facade is a lie
Hiding a storm inside

Terrifying is the beast awakened
Its glimmering white teeth
Shining your reflection
Its striated muscle
Twitches just beneath skin
Holding all that power in

If the thought makes you tremble lightly
Heart rate increasing slightly
Imagine how it feels
Eye to eye to face the beast
Blind fury within reach
Black rage unleashed
On all that surrounds
There's no backing down

Shhhh, keep it passively encaged
Don't poke the beast tempting fate
Give it a reason to break through chains
Four centuries of pent up rage

Will finally have its day
Head & limbs scattered
Bones & skull shattered
When we unleash
The wrath of the beast.

*Corrupt Mission*
You should have never been
In a land that's foreign
Misuse of forces
Snatching precious resources
You cut off the head of state
To insert your snake
A puppet on a string acting on command
In the exploitation play you make

Instead of letting the people be
In charge of their own destiny
You bring in your fuckery
Spreading false Christianity
In the name of democracy
Permanent occupation
You abort the cause
When the cost gets too much
Claiming, "Mission Accomplished"

Spreading lies, abandoning your allies
To be assassinated
When the insurgents come surging in
To fill the void you leave behind
Where is the aid
For the humanitarian crisis
That you create
You leave the people high & dry
While your planes take off to fly
Bodies falling from the sky

There is no democratic union
Only chaos & confusion
Dominion was the mission

Motivated by capitalist greed
Spreading sickness & disease
In the name of manifest destiny.

## *Refuge*

One tribe from many
Sharing what we can carry
In a foreign realm far from home
Born possessing nothing of our own
We grow to love our people more than things
Our shades of melanin
Under the perpetual threat of violent action
With each sunrise we wake to face hostility
We take refuge in our community
Coarse hands & barefeet work the land
Back breaking labor so others can eat
The colonizer reaps the benefit of our sowed seeds
Despised, chastised, no tears in our eyes
We cannot afford to waste the water crying
Life's important lessons
Our treasure cannot be bartered or sold
We cling to our kinfolk
Their laughter is cherished more than silver & gold
Suffering long on a diasporic journey
Our language is sung in blue notes
Melancholic melodies telling tales of a lost nomadic tribe
Wandering the desert in search of oasis
Displaced Africans from war zones & slave ships
Forced relocation to tent camps & tenement projects
Some of the deepest souls you are blessed to meet
Impart wisdom more ancient than boab trees
Bare witness to parables told around the fire ring
Soulful hymns sung from the heart of the refugee

He speaks prophetically as his guitar gently weeps
Longing for home, singing of peace.

## *No More Struggle*

Why are we fighting so hard to be equal & free
When we can just live in perfect peace
In a land that was always meant to be

This country is not ours
They offer our people no justice
This is just where our historic trauma lives
Where captors refuse to take part in any healing reconciliation
So the cycle of abuse is stuck repeating

Let's say we do the work & unify
Gain collective knowledge of self
The system is designed to keep us in chains
The most probable outcome is a life fighting

For freedom to live unequally
In this capitalist rat race
Forever chasing paper dreams
But never finding peace
Is it worth it?

I now believe that Black America will never be free
But our inheritance
Our ancestors died for
Bought & paid for with their blood & tears
Gives us access that others would trade their world to gain

We should collect what's owed
Take our pot of gold
Back to the motherland
To build a Wakanda
Where our roots run deep in the soil

With dual citizenship
We travel as we please
The best of the east & the west
A tribe of nomadic world citizens
Free by true definition

Keep an open mind friend
It doesn't matter which country
Our people run the continent
Make a pilgrimage to connect
Gain some perspective

It's a spiritual experience coming home
That I didn't search for or expect
But when it hit me it was vibrational healing
Profoundly life changing, amazing

I want that for my seed
Giving him options
To move freely
In a land where his existence isn't in question
Human rights threatened

We can't make demands
Before we convince ourselves
Dismantling 400 years of institutional oppression
That continues on every level of our system
Is a monster in & of itself

Exiting while Black isn't giving up
It's gaining access to a life beyond limits
The peace & security to exist as a whole citizen
Psalm 119 point me in the right direction
I'm going home.

## *No Mix Up*

Don't call me *mixed*
There was no mix up in my conception
My blackness
Isn't some watered down version

Do you think it matters
To anyone but us
Where do you think
Calculating percentages comes from

The Master Plan
Still at work within
Constructed to divide & conquer
Don't let them win

My heritage
Is not in question
All they ever see
Is kinky hair & dark complexion

Our bloodline holds the DNA
Of all kinds since ancient times
Making our melanin
So beautifully varying

Travel to the Motherland to discover your origin
It will blow your mind to find
We possess every hair texture
Coupled with all shades of melanated skin

Our power is in unison
Let's stop the measuring
Comparison & confusion

There exists no mixed human
When race is an illusion.

### *Blaxit*

It's a mass exodus when black & brown kin
Realize they're still captive
Under the flag of fake freedom

It's time to leave the game
To struggle is not competition
The score is rigged
To make sure we don't win

Taxation without representation
Police brutality
False imprisonment
Housing discrimination

We advocate for reparations
What is their motivation
To end a system of oppression
They still benefit from

Wasting our lives waiting for wrong to make it right
We understand the assignment
It's time to #blaxit
To our ancestral land in pursuit of higher vibration

Reclaiming our time
Take our talent & ingenuity
Knowledge & wealth
To invest in a tribe where together we thrive

We are all Africans
The table is set for us to feast
Mama is calling her sons & daughters
To make our journey east.

## *African Renewed*

I sit on a cliff at Cape Point
Watching the cool blue of the Atlantic
Dance with the gem colored warmth of the Indian Ocean

As I meditate
I feel the weight of the entire continent
Bearing down on my back
In all its glorious enormity

I sense the blood of my people deep in the land
Their vibrational energy emanates from the rock
The waves are crashing & I hear distant chanting

An empath channeling with high frequency
In this sacred space
My openness is on 10
In a tidal wave of emotion my awareness comes surging in

All at once I absorb the deepest anguish
Felt when my ancestors were shackled & whipped onto wooden ships
Crammed naked by force into its giant belly
I can smell the suffocating odor of massive death

The savagery & trauma recorded in our DNA is excruciating
Tears stream down my face
In both heartbreak & deep cleansing healing
None of them could imagine the horrors that awaited
Across the Middle Passage

400 years
Let that sink in
Resonate
Four centuries

It took to completely erase
Our names
Our stories, our language, our song

Who could dream
The descendants of family stolen
Never to be heard from again
Would one day cross the vast ocean to return

Without written knowledge
All that remains is spirit
The map has been divided up
Lines drawn & redrawn
By Europeans in an attempt to stake their claims

Original Africans were explorers
The entire continent traversed
Trading up & down rivers & following animal migrations
They moved with the season in harmonic synergy

Community was an ever changing presence
If it sounds familiar
It's because our behavior echoes tradition
They can rewrite history
Our blood is thicker than their textbooks

My tribe are global citizens
Spread throughout the diaspora
We can come together everywhere as kin
Instant family

In this moment
I feel my ancestors rejoicing
Their love surges all around me

Surrounding me

They call me daughter in my ancestral name
Etched in salt crystals carried by the sea breeze
I am fully conscious of who I am & where I belong
My spirit awakens, I am home.

*Fin*

# POET'S CORNER

GianMarie is a poet, entrepreneur & mother. Born & raised in the Midwest, she fell in love with spoken word art at a young age. By the time she moved out East at seventeen to attend university at a HBCU, the Neo Soul Movement of the 1990s was in full swing. Inspired by the artistry of heavy hitters like Jill Scott & the legendary Nina Simone, GianMarie took her poetry to open mic night. She has said that she felt most alive while on stage blessing the mic accompanied by live instrumentation.

GianMarie kept dreaming through her poetry, putting pen to paper over two decades until 2011 when *Black Girl Daydreamin* became a reality. Like so many anointed black creatives, GianMarie let the art take a backseat out of necessity to work, pay bills & eat.

Life & love brought her to the West Coast where she found her forever tribe walking the hills in Berkeley, California. Elevated by the entrepreneurial vibe of the East Bay, the activism of the Black Lives Matter movement, & inspired by the pure artistic soul that comes alive in Oakland, GianMarie compiled a fresh collection of poetry. *Soul Anthropology* was released in 2021, a long awaited follow up to her first collection of poetry.

Self-published & available worldwide for digital & print readers, GianMarie states that her poetry isn't about turning a profit. For her, the work is released & made affordable, so that everyone has access. Too often the people's suffering is endured in silence. GianMarie's motivating desire is to give the struggle, trauma, love & dreams of her tribe a voice.

GianMarie is currently working on her fourth release, a fresh collection of poetry expected to be available in 2024. Continue the journey with GianMarie by following her blog & poetry page to be the first to know when new poetry is released: https://www.gianmariepoetry.com